Bo was a father. He had a baby son.

He didn't know anything about babies or being a dad. His father hadn't been much of a father, and he did not doubt that Hans would say that he hadn't been much of a son either...

Now wasn't the time to dig into his complicated history with his father; he needed to focus on the here and now.

"Do you know how to look after a baby, Mr. Sørenson?"

He didn't have the first clue. "No," he admitted.

"Do you have any family members who could help you?"

Bo thought about his mother—dressed in designer clothes, her blond hair perfect and her nails freshly painted—trying to change Matheo's diaper. Nope, that wasn't going to happen. Bridget would be horrified by the latest addition to their family. Well, *horrified* was a strong word. *Uninterested* or *unaffected* would be a better choice.

"No."

"Then I suggest you hire a nanny."

Joss Wood loves books and traveling—especially to the wild places of southern Africa and, well, anywhere. She's a wife, a mom to two teenagers and a slave to two cats. After a career in local economic development, she now writes full-time. Joss is a member of Romance Writers of America and Romance Writers of South Africa.

Books by Joss Wood

Harlequin Presents

Cape Town Tycoons

The Nights She Spent with the CEO
The Baby Behind Their Marriage Merger

Scandals of the Le Roux Wedding

The Billionaire's One-Night Baby
The Powerful Boss She Craves
The Twin Secret She Must Reveal

Harlequin Desire

Just a Little Jilted
Their Temporary Arrangement
The Trouble with Little Secrets
Keep Your Enemies Close...

Visit the Author Profile page
at Harlequin.com for more titles.

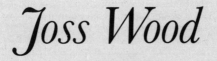

Joss Wood

HIRED FOR THE BILLIONAIRE'S SECRET SON

PRESENTS

ℍ HARLEQUIN®
PRESENTS™

Recycling programs
for this product may
not exist in your area.

ISBN-13: 978-1-335-59299-6

Hired for the Billionaire's Secret Son

Copyright © 2023 by Joss Wood

For questions and comments about the quality of this book, please contact us at CustomerService@Harlequin.com.

Harlequin Enterprises ULC
22 Adelaide St. West, 41st Floor
Toronto, Ontario M5H 4E3, Canada
www.Harlequin.com

Printed in U.S.A.

HIRED FOR THE BILLIONAIRE'S SECRET SON

CHAPTER ONE

I'm sorry, but I am currently out of the office on my summer vacation and will only be checking my emails on a limited basis.

Bo Sørenson scowled at his monitor and wondered whether the whole of Denmark was on vacation and whether he was the only sap working. He looked through the glass walls of his office and scowled at the free seats—his staff didn't have dedicated desks but picked their work station depending on their mood and task—and the lack of activity. Normally, he had people walking in and out of his office, asking questions, looking for guidance on a technical question, bouncing an idea off him or needing his approval for a staff hire or out-of-the-norm expenditure.

Here, on the third floor of the building he owned situated on Copenhagen's North Harbour, was his favourite place to be. He and the rest of the office staff employed by Sørenson Yachts, designs and builders, occupied the third floor of the modern building—the vessels were constructed at their boatyard in Skagen. The lines of the building were inspired by a cruise ship, and the floor-to-ceiling windows let in as much natural light as possible.

While his office might resemble a graveyard in summer, on the plus side, it was a great time for him to knuckle down and catch up with his design work. He had a long waiting list of exceptionally wealthy clients and corporations waiting for a Bo Sørenson-designed vessel. Sometimes that was a kick-ass yacht suitable for an oligarch, sometimes it was a racing yacht, sometimes it was a simple but incredibly luxurious wooden sailing boat. Regardless of the type of vessel, every design would reflect his love of clean lines, modern and unfussy but exceptionally detailed.

And the owner would have the bragging rights of saying it was a Bo Sørenson design. He'd worked all hours of the day for the past fifteen years to distinguish himself from his father and grandfather, both of whom were world-famous designers, and he finally felt that the yachting world no longer believed he was riding their coattails. It wasn't easy to distinguish yourself when you were the son of a genius who'd died far too young and who, they said, had never reached his full potential—and who had been the bad boy virtuoso of the maritime world.

Bo spun round in his ergonomic chair and looked at the framed photograph of his father standing on the *Miss Bea*, the first racing yacht Malte had designed, the wind blowing his thick blond hair. As everyone told him, Bo was the spitting image of his father and, if he never had to hear the expression 'two peas in a pod' again, it would be too soon. Yes, they were both tall, blond and fit, and he had his father's green eyes and rugged face, but that was where the similarities ended.

Unlike his father, Bo was a workaholic and didn't spend the year hopping from one glamorous yachting spot to another—from Monaco to Costa Smeralda to Dubai—redeeming himself by occasionally producing ground-breaking, innovative designs.

Yes, the patents from those designs had allowed him to be the *enfant terrible* of the yachting world, and brought kudos and opportunity to Sørenson Yachts. But, in Bo's eyes, he'd wasted his talent and spent far too much time being frivolous. And maybe, if he'd partied less and stayed home more, Bo would have more memories of him than him sweeping in, ruffling his hair, handing him a present and sweeping out again, desperate to leave them behind, desperate for the next adventure—and the next woman.

As the years passed, Malte's visits diminished to once or twice a year and Bo watched his mother become more bitter, more emotionally distant, colder and harder. By the time he was a teenager, Bridget had morphed into a brittle, robotic creature who'd been more his bank manager and boss than his mother.

Bridget, who'd been determined that he did not follow in Malte's footsteps, had pushed him hard. If she'd had her way, she would've kept him from his paternal grandfather but neither Bo, nor Asger, would've tolerated her coming between them. He'd loved his stoic and silent grandfather, the one adult who seemed to enjoy his company. Bridget had been bitterly disappointed when he'd taken an engineering degree, specialised in yacht design and joined the family business under his grandfather as owner and CEO.

Within the first year of joining the company that had been in his family for seventy-five years, Bo realised that his grandfather's grip on the company, and reality, was slipping. As he'd taken over many of Asger's responsibilities, Bo discovered that his father's contribution to the company did not justify his enormous salary.

At the age of twenty-four, Bo had realised that Sørenson Yachts was on the verge of collapsing and knew that he had to do something or the company started by his grandfather—the man he respected and who was, mentally, fading away—would go bankrupt. It was up to him to save it. Bo's mum had the emotional range of a puppet, but she was a highly successful businesswoman who'd made a fortune in import and export. With her, Bo had wooed investors and, in the nick of time, put together a deal that had not only given him managerial control of Sørenson Yachts—Asger had given him his power of attorney—but had also injected a healthy amount of cash into the then-failing company.

It had also made him his father's boss. His father hadn't been happy about the board appointing him as his grandfather's successor, and had been furious when his son cut his exorbitant salary and cancelled his company credit cards. He'd been livid when Bo demanded his presence in the office and gave him deadlines for projects he needed to complete.

Malte had lasted six months and, on the day his dad resigned, the anvil resting on Bo's chest lifted. The company was his to do with once he took control, and was in the driver's seat.

But life, as it had the habit to do, wiped away his self-congratulations. His grandfather had died from a massive stroke and, just a few weeks later, his father slammed his newly purchased McLaren into a concrete barrier and died on impact.

Bo had been named as both their heirs, and he had sole ownership of Sørenson Yachts—something he'd dreamed of, but it had come at a cost. In what seemed to be the blink of an eye, more than half his family had been wiped out— a man he'd adored and a man he hadn't—and Bo understood, on a fundamental level, his mother's desire to keep her emotional distance. When feelings were invited to the party, they caused havoc—grief and loss when you loved someone, regret, anger and frustration when you didn't.

No, it was far easier to live his life solo, having bed-based relationships and keeping all relationships superficial. He had sporting friends, guys whose company he enjoyed, but he knew far more about their lives than they did his. He had lovers, not girlfriends or partners, and his sexual partners knew not to expect anything more from him than a good time in bed.

He had lunch with his mother once a month, and they spent ninety minutes discussing their mutual businesses. Her business was her favourite child, giving her everything she needed. She'd never been able to juggle being a businesswoman and a mother, and he'd suffered for it. One of the reasons why he eschewed having a wife and a family was because he never again wanted to feel like he or his children were less important than his or his partner's career.

He was sure that there were people out there who had the work-life balance figured out, but he preferred not to take the chance of being left behind emotionally. He knew what loneliness and parental lack of interest felt like, how busy and uninterested parents could scar a child. Having a partner and child would force him to redesign his working life, something he wasn't interested in doing. And, because he was only ever attracted to smart, ambitious women, he knew that a relationship with a career-orientated woman would mean putting him, or any child they had, in the position of begging for her time, interest and affection. A person only had so much to give and, as he knew, a business demanded a large portion of one's energy.

He preferred not to fight to be seen, heard or paid attention to.

Bo stood up and stretched, annoyed at his uncharacteristic bout of introspection. He had work to do, designs to start and designs to complete. He would spend the summer working, but that wasn't anything new; he got anxious and irritable when he was doing, and achieving. He only had a certain amount of time on this earth, and he intended to leave a legacy behind. Legacies weren't made by sitting on beaches sipping cocktails or lounging around reading. Legacies took work and work was what he did best.

An hour later, Bo was working at his drafting board, deep in the zone, his entire focus on the design of a high-tech racing yacht to compete in the Sydney Cup in 2026. It was a new concept, something that would hopefully revolutionise competitive sailing. He'd been concentrating so deeply that it took him ages to hear the knock on his door and, when he looked up, his junior receptionist stood on the other side of the door, a worried-looking, middle-aged woman standing behind her.

He walked across his expansive office and opened the door, wondering why he was being disturbed when he'd left strict instructions that he wasn't to be.

'Mr Sørenson, this is Mrs Daniels. She urgently needs to speak to you.'

'Make an appointment,' he told the woman, his voice sharp. 'I'm designing and I can't be distracted.'

Mrs Daniels, with sharp blue eyes, was not impressed by his curt statement. 'What I have to say can't wait, Mr Sørenson. And, unless you want me to discuss your private matters in front of your staff member, you'd best let me come in.'

He didn't have private matters to discuss. His last

one-night stand had been a few weeks ago and he lived alone. He didn't have any brothers or sisters and his mother was as self-reliant and -contained as he was. He saw the curiosity on his receptionist's face and instructed Agnes to return to her work. He jerked his head, gesturing for the older woman to follow him into his office. He closed the door behind her and lifted his eyebrows. He had an intimidating face; people said that he could look scary, but it was his face, so what could he do? And, if it made her get to the point quicker, all the better. He had work to do.

'I work for Social Services, Mr Sørenson,' Mrs Daniels said, lowering her tote bag to the floor and clutching a brown, official-looking file to her chest.

So? What on earth could she want with him?

Mrs Daniels opened the file and looked down, her eyes scanning the documentation. 'Miss Christianson… Daniella Christianson…do you know her?'

Dani? Sure. He nodded. 'We had a brief relationship about eighteen months ago.' Though calling their three-week affair a relationship was stretching it—they'd had a couple of dinners and a lot of sex.

'I regret to tell you that Ms Christianson died a few days ago.'

Bo rubbed his lower jaw, shock running through his system. He'd met Daniella at a cocktail party and she'd been fun and vibrant, a tall Brazilian bombshell. Just a few years younger than himself, she'd been taking a six-month sabbatical in Copenhagen and had been both smart and sexy. 'I hadn't heard—I am sorry to hear that.' He was, but he didn't understand why a social worker was delivering the news.

'What happened?' Bo asked, unable to believe that someone so vibrant was no more.

'It was a car accident outside Rio de Janeiro.'

Mrs Daniels nailed him with a direct look. 'Were you aware that Ms Christianson was recently married, and that her husband was planning on adopting her son?'

'Why would I be? As I said, I haven't spoken to her for well over a year,' Bo replied.

'So she didn't tell you that you are the father of her son?'

Wait! What?

Bo felt his knees dissolve just a little and quickly decided that he hadn't heard her correctly. He didn't have a son.

Mrs Daniels grabbed a visitor's chair, shoved it behind his knees and Bo gratefully sank into it. Gripping the arms of the chair, he looked up, seeing a little sympathy in her blue eyes. 'I have a son?'

'Judging by your stunned reaction, I'm assuming you didn't know?'

'No, I had no idea. I haven't had any contact with Daniella since I called it done,' he told her. 'She left to go back to Brazil a month later and, no, she didn't tell me she was pregnant!'

But that could be because he'd made it very clear to her—as he made it clear to all his lovers—that he wasn't interested in long-term commitment or children.

'From what I gathered from her grandmother, her

husband was her boyfriend from college and they reconnected when she was pregnant. They married and he wanted to raise the boy as his own.'

Okay. 'But he also died?'

Mrs Daniels nodded. 'The baby was also in the crash, but he came away unharmed.'

Dear Lord. Bo rested his forearms on his thighs, idly noticing that his hands were trembling. 'The baby's birth was registered in Brazil, but he has been returned to Denmark. She put you as his father and you are now responsible for him.'

'I am?'

'Mrs Christianson's husband's family has no legal claim to the child—the adoption papers weren't filed yet and, frankly, none of them is in a position to look after a nine-month-old child. Mrs Christianson is survived by her grandmother, who cannot look after the child either. He's yours to raise.'

But…

What was happening here? How had he gone from living his life solo, from eschewing relationships, to having a son? And how was it that Daniella had fallen pregnant by him? He was obsessively careful about using condoms.

He needed to ask. 'How can you be sure he's mine?' Bo asked. 'I'm a pretty careful guy.'

'Even though she never told you, you are named on his birth certificate as his father. And, even though he is very young, the resemblance between you is quite startling,' Mrs Daniels replied. 'But, if you require a DNA test for your peace of mind, that's your right. It will mean that he will stay with his foster family until the matter is settled.'

'He's with a foster family?' Bo asked. What he knew about babies was minimal, and he knew even less about the Social Services system, but he'd watched enough movies to be sceptical that the baby was being well cared for. He was probably wrong, but he didn't like the idea of the baby—his son?—being in a tumultuous environment.

'Since he arrived in Copenhagen last week, yes. The foster family is very nice, one of our best, but they are not a long-term solution,' Mrs Daniels stated. 'Living with you is.'

Bo swallowed and ran his hands over his face. 'Do I have any choice about raising him?'

Mrs Daniels's eyes cooled, and he caught the disappointment in them and felt three feet tall. 'We could arrange to have him adopted, if having a child would be such an imposition on your life, Mr Sørenson. That's an option.'

She wasn't impressed by him, and she didn't need to explain why. He came from one of the best and most well-known families in the country and he had money. He sounded like a self-centred idiot, someone who was more concerned about how this child would affect his life than about the welfare of his son.

He sounded like his own father and that was unacceptable.

Bo stood up and slid his hands into the pockets of his casual grey trousers, bunching his fists. 'And you say that he looks like me?' he asked, hoping she heard the apology and embarrassment in his voice. He rarely apologised, and he also didn't want this woman thinking badly of him, but he suspected that ship had sailed.

'What is his name, by the way?' Bo added, thinking that he couldn't keep calling his son 'him'.

'His name is Matheo, spelt in the Danish way. And he looks exactly like you,' she told him. 'Same eyes, same, nose, same chin. He's a big boy so I suspect he'll also have your height.'

Bo blew air over his lips and tried to find some moisture in his mouth. 'I genuinely don't know what to think or say.'

For the first time, Mrs Daniels smiled. 'I've just handed you life-changing news—it's a lot to take in. But, unfortunately, we do need to move forward as quickly as possible. Matheo needs to get settled in a permanent environment. His needs are the only ones that matter.'

Yes, he got that. But he was rocked to his core. This stranger was telling him he had a child, something he'd never planned. He was the product of a horrible marriage between two wholly unsuited people. He'd vowed that he'd never risk putting a child through the trauma of being caught between a cold mother and a volatile father. The only way to guarantee that never happened—accepting that anyone could change their minds about having children at any point—was to stay single, unmarried and unattached.

But now he was a father, something he'd never

considered. He'd discovered the delights of a female body in his mid-teens but, even as a young man, he'd understood that babies were a consequence of sex and he'd been ultra-careful about using protection. He'd never trusted any of his sexual partners enough to leave the issue of contraception in their hands, so he made sure to protect them both. Damn, how *had* this happened? Well, he understood the mechanics, he just didn't understand why his life had gone off-piste like this. Though, to be fair, so had little Matheo's.

'I have a photograph of him, if you'd like to see it,' Mrs Daniels offered.

He nodded, unable to speak past the lump in his throat. Bo waited, the fire ants of impatience crawling under his skin as he watched her look in her bag for her phone. She pulled it out, took another few minutes to find her glasses and then it took her ten years for her to find the picture she was looking for. Mrs Daniels thrust the phone at him, and he took it gingerly, hauling air into his lungs as he looked down.

Bo's world stopped as he looked down into that all too familiar face. He didn't need the DNA test; Matheo looked exactly as he had at the same age. As the social worker had said, his son looked a lot like him, and he could see little of Dani in his face. He was a Sørenson through and through, with eyes as deep a green as his.

'If you put our baby photographs together, I would be hard-pressed to tell you which one was of him and which one was of me,' Bo admitted, shoving a shaky hand into his hair.

'Do you need to sit down again?'

He managed a small smile. 'No, I'm fine. What's the next step?' He needed to focus on the practicalities, what happened next. He could panic later.

'So you want to do the DNA testing?'

'No, it's not necessary. The dates are right, and he looks exactly like I did as a child. I'll take him.'

Bo winced, knowing he'd made Matheo sound like a puppy left out in the rain. He hadn't meant to; it was just so difficult to think, to wrap his head around this stunning news. He was a father—he had a baby son. He didn't know anything about babies or being a dad. His dad hadn't been much of a father, and he did not doubt that Malte would say that he hadn't been much of a son either...

Now wasn't the time to dig into his complicated history with his father; he needed to focus on the here and now.

'Do you know how to look after a baby, Mr Sørenson?'

He didn't have the first clue. 'No,' he admitted.

'Do you have any family members who could help you?'

Bo thought about his mother trying to change Matheo's nappy, dressed in Chanel or Balenciaga, her blonde hair perfect and her nails freshly painted. Nope, that wasn't going to happen. Bridget would be horrified by the latest addition to their family. Well, 'horrified' was a strong word—uninterested or un-affected would be a better choice.

'No.'

'Then I suggest you hire a nanny; there are several reputable agencies who can send you some help.'

Right, that was a good suggestion. He would need someone not only to look after Matheo but to teach him how to look after Matheo. How to make bottles and bath a toddler, how to put on a nappy. It couldn't be that hard, but having someone show him the ropes would make life so much easier. 'I have money—I could hire the best in the world,' he told Mrs Daniels, not caring if he sounded like an over-confident git. 'Where do I find the best nanny I can?'

'Sabine du Foy runs a very good agency out of Paris,' she replied. 'Expensive but, so I've heard, worth every cent.'

Bo walked over to his draft board and scribbled the name onto his drawing. He'd just ruined his work, but that was the least of his problems. 'Would they be able to get someone here quickly?'

The social worker shrugged. 'Call her and find out. When you have a nanny in place, I'll arrange to bring Matheo to you.'

Right—bring Matheo. To him…to live…for ever.

Bo felt the need to sit down again.

CHAPTER TWO

IN BERLIN, OLLIE COOPER removed a handful of lingerie from her dresser drawer and dumped it on her bed, thinking that, with so much practice, her packing process should be a lot more streamlined than it was.

Ollie was moving on, unexpectedly and two months sooner than she'd thought. After just four weeks of a three-month contract working as a nanny to a ten- and twelve-year-old—the sons of a dotcom millionaire and his ex-model American wife—she was no longer needed. They loved her, she was told, but an unexpected opportunity had arisen in the US, quite close to family, and they wouldn't require as much help over there as they did here. She'd be paid for the full three months, and they were sorry.

Ollie was sorry too; she now had an empty eight weeks before she had to return to London and she had no idea how to fill them. This was her last nanny assignment, and she felt both sad and glad, anxious and relieved. She didn't want to work as a nanny any more, but she didn't want to leave the role entirely.

She loved kids, she really did, but it was hard not to get attached, to keep her emotional distance. Not becoming too involved was why she'd swapped from long-term contracts to short-term assignments. She couldn't allow herself to become overly entangled in her charges' lives.

She'd done that with Becca and it'd nearly killed her. Watching the life fade from that bright, magical, stunning little soul had pushed her to the limits of her mental endurance and, after she'd passed, she'd realised that she needed to cultivate distance, to keep a barrier, for her mental health. The easiest way to do that was to limit the time she spent with her charges. The down side of the arrangement was that, just as she started to get to know the children, to understand their quirks and foibles, she left their lives. It was sad, and sometimes there were tears, but she walked away with her heart intact.

Normally she knew exactly where she was going, and would have a dossier on her next family from Sabine's agency, and familiarise herself with her charges. Not knowing where to go was a strange experience for her. For the first time in five years, she didn't have a job lined up or a family to help out.

You knew this time was coming, Cooper. It might be two months earlier than you envisioned but it shouldn't be a shock. You've had your five years of freedom and it's time for you to honour the deal you made.

But, technically, not until the first day of September, which was still a little way off.

The fact was, she was running out of time, and Ollie felt as though she was facing the guillotine. A bit dramatic, but she couldn't think of anything worse than going back to London and sitting behind a desk every day. She would rather watch paint dry.

But she'd made a deal, and her parents set a lot of store by their children keeping their word—as they should.

Ollie looked around the gorgeous apartment she'd been using for the past few weeks and sighed at the mess she'd made. There were clothes on the bed, make-up scattered on the dresser and books she needed to box. Her family had left for the States yesterday and she needed to be out of here in two days—that was when the estate agents would hand over the keys to the new owner. She needed to make a decision: should she go back to London, take a long holiday that would make a dent in her savings, or should she take another quick assignment if she could find one?

Bored with packing and feeling anxious, Ollie picked up her mobile and walked onto the balcony overlooking the mansion's tiny garden, and beyond the tall hedge a small park. She'd spent a lot of time in that park, kicking a football around with the boys, or jogging round it before the boys woke up and the craziness of the day had begun. Ollie dialled the number of the agency she worked for and, on request, was immediately put through to Sabine, the agency's owner.

Switching to French—Ollie spoke four languages

fluently—she greeted her boss and spent the next few minutes catching up with the woman, who was not only her boss but her friend and mentor. Sabine had suggested on more than one occasion that she buy into the agency as a junior partner, as Ollie was the only other person she could imagine running her precious business. There was nothing Ollie wanted more—she could see herself in the role of matching nannies and au pairs with families, ironing out issues and expanding the business—but first she had to fulfil her promise to her parents.

She filled Sabine in on her client's abrupt departure, to find that Sabine had already been informed. 'They've already paid me, and I paid you, for the full three months, although you've only worked for them for four weeks.'

'So what's your plan for the immediate future?' Sabine asked with her usual dose of French pragmatism.

'I've got to be back in London at the end of August,' Ollie told her. 'I don't know what I should do between now and then.'

'You could take a holiday,' Sabine suggested.

Ollie wrinkled her nose. Doing nothing for a few days would be nice but she'd soon get bored.

While she wasn't a workaholic, being productive was important to her. She'd seen how hard her father and mother had had to work to build their accountancy practice into the behemoth it was today and, like her brothers, she'd inherited their work ethic. She didn't like being idle and doing nothing—though sometimes 'nothing' was what her family thought she did.

Maybe that wasn't fair. They loved her; they just wished she did something a little more conventional. Her mum, especially, found it exceptionally difficult to reconcile the idea of her smart, *educated* daughter supervising homework, changing nappies or wiping snotty noses. No one in her family realised that she was one of the best rewarded nannies in the business and that she had a list of influential families, ranging from nobility to celebrities to sports icons, who wanted her to look after their little darlings. She had a reputation for excellence and the families who could afford her services wanted her. '*My daughter, the nanny* didn't have the same cachet as '*my daughter, the accountant*'.

'Maybe I should do another two-month stint,' Ollie suggested to Sabine, rubbing her fingertips across her forehead.

'You mean you'd rather find another short-term assignment than return to London early in case your family figures out, from your morbid face and droopy lips, that you would rather pull out your toenails with pliers than work as one of their accountants?'

That was it, in a nutshell.

A natural student, Ollie had won a place to study accountancy, following her parents and brothers into the field. But, two years into her degree, she'd come to realise that she'd made a mistake and that she was wholly unsuited to becoming an accountant. But she was too far in to switch courses, according to her family, and she needed to stick it out. So she'd gritted her teeth and ploughed through; luckily she hadn't found the work overly onerous and it had made her family happy.

They'd been less happy—as in, furious—when she'd told them that she had no intention of joining the family firm and that she wanted to travel. After many arguments, they'd worked out a deal: she could travel and do her own thing for five years but then she'd have to return to London or Johannesburg and work in one of the Cooper & Co branches for five years so that they could get some benefit, and a return on, the very expensive investment they'd made in her education.

If she didn't, then they'd all have to accept what she already suspected: that she'd wasted her education. Her parents would find that very hard to forgive.

Her degree was from the London School of Economics and, as a non-UK resident, it had cost them a bundle to send her to one of the most prestigious universities in the UK. In their eyes, she'd been playing at being a nanny for the past five years—it was time for her to settle down into a career and use her degree.

Her parents put the highest possible value on education and she and her brothers had been raised to believe that a university degree was not a right, but a privilege, and never to be taken for granted. She already felt guilty for not using her degree for the past five years and loathed the idea of wasting her time and efforts. But mostly, Ollie couldn't stand the fact that she might've wasted her parent's money.

No, she had to fulfil the terms of their deal and go back. She would white-knuckle her way through the next five years. Unfortunately, Ollie knew that, within a year of working for them, her family would also start pressurising her to get married and have babies. They wanted it all for her—a stunning career, a successful husband and for her to be a mother.

Ollie wasn't that interested in any of the above. She wasn't an accountant; the thought made her break out in hives. Her parents had a super-strong, amazing marriage, the type of marriage everyone aspired to. She wanted what they had but modern life, modern people, didn't manage marriages like that any more. That had been proved to her by her ex-fiancé, who'd had the emotional depth of a dirty puddle and the inability to keep his fly zipped, and she refused to settle for less than her parents had. As for having children, well, she'd had Becca, and she knew what it was like to love and then lose a kid.

No, she wasn't interested in being dismissed, ignored and cheated on again and she never wanted to be as emotionally involved with a child as she'd been with Becca. It hurt too much. She'd rather live alone, be alone, loving from a distance.

'You're right; I don't particularly want to go back to London early. I'd have to live with them while I look for a flat and I'd be pressurised to start work early. A vacation will take a chunk out of my savings. Do you have a couple of teenagers who need looking after for the summer?'

'Most parents with any sense have made their arrangements already, Ollie,' Sabine told her.

Yes, she knew that it was a bit late in the day to pick up last-minute work. 'I know; I just didn't expect my assignment to finish early.'

Now that she was faced with going home, she wasn't ready and really didn't want to do it. Spending two months in Goa doing nothing was rapidly becoming an attractive option.

Ollie heard the tap of Sabine's nails against her keyboard. 'A request did come in yesterday afternoon. A single father in Denmark needs a nanny for a nine-month-old baby. I told him that finding a permanent nanny will take some time, but he's so desperate he'll take anyone. I didn't think of you because, a, you were heading home, b, you were already committed in Berlin and, c, you prefer to work with older children.'

She didn't dislike babies—they were cute enough—but older kids, toddlers and up, were so much more fun. 'Tell me more about him,' Ollie said, sitting on the edge of her bed. She preferred to work for a couple or single mums. The one single dad she'd worked for at the start of her career had seemed to think that she'd provide additional services as well as looking after his two very precocious children. She'd reported him to Sabine, and he was no longer able to access nannies from Sabine's agency. That kind of behaviour was not tolerated by her.

'He's a yacht designer and builder and, unexpectedly, has gained custody of his nine-month-old son,' Sabine explained. 'He wants someone to help teach him how to care for a baby—he has zero experience—and we've also been tasked with finding him a long-term nanny.'

Most parents prepared themselves for the arrival of a baby, but this father hadn't. Why not? Colour her intrigued.

'And you say he's in Copenhagen?' Copenhagen in summer was supposedly gorgeous and she'd never spent any length of time in the city. It might be… interesting.

'He's offering above the normal rate, as he needs someone to help with the baby and show him what to do. He readily admits to not having a clue,' Sabine stated.

'I'm interested in the job, Sabine. I'm not crazy that it's a single dad, but I'm not twenty-two any more, and I could shut down any unwanted attention a lot quicker, and with more confidence, if it occurred.'

'Are you sure?' Sabine asked.

She was very sure that she wasn't ready to go back to London yet. 'Sure-ish,' she said. 'Send him my CV and see if he's interested.'

If he was, then they could do a video-conference call. 'But he'd have to make up his mind fairly quickly because I have to be out of this place the day after tomorrow.'

'You could always come to Paris and stay with me for a bit,' Sabine offered.

She could. But she knew that, if this job didn't pan out, then it was the universe's way of telling her that she needed to go home and face the music.

'I will call him and see what he says,' Sabine told her. 'I'll send you his file too.'

'That sounds like a plan,' Ollie agreed. 'Speak soon, yeah?'

Forty-five minutes later, before she'd had time to read the man's file, Ollie heard back from Sabine. She had an interview in Copenhagen the day after next, and she was to come prepared to start work immediately. If she wasn't successful in securing the position—and that wasn't likely, because this Bo Sørenson was desperate—he'd pay for her flight to any European destination. He was impressed by her references, he needed her and had offered to pay double her usual rate to secure her services to look after his son.

For Ollie, it was an offer she couldn't refuse. And a way to delay the inevitable.

Copenhagen in summer was a city filled with sunshine, busy with tourists and everyone seemed to be on a bike. As she made her way through the city, Ollie took in the juxtaposition between the grand old buildings and the sleek lines of modern architecture, the old and new cohabiting happily together.

It was bursting with cafés, shops, great-looking people and some of the best restaurants in the world.

Honestly, there were worst places to be, and unless her new boss turned out to be a total prat this would be where she would stay for the next two months. How exciting!

She had plans to discover what made this city tick on her off days, which were written into her contract. She wanted to take a boat tour and see the city from the water, hire a bicycle, meander down the side streets or take a walking tour, sampling Danish pastries and *smørrebrød*—an apparently delicious open sandwich—along the way. She'd heard about Reffen, an organic street-food market and urban area that had a reputation for innovation and sustainability and she wanted to explore that part of the city.

Oh, she wanted to explore it all—the sights, sounds, smells and food. So far, the city was looking good.

She hoped her new boss would be good too.

Ollie glanced down at her phone and re-read the message she'd received from Sabine fifteen minutes ago. She'd spoken with Mr Sørenson this morning and, despite him having met Matheo, the Danish Social Services were saying that Matheo would only be moved from his foster family into his father's care when she was in situ. Her eyebrows had raised when she'd realised that this was at Mr Sørenson's request. Was he so inexperienced that he couldn't look after a baby for a night, or did he only have his son's best interests at heart? Or both?

Time would tell.

Ollie watched as her taxi driver negotiated the

streets of the city, her eyebrows raising when he whistled his appreciation as the car crawled down what he told her was one of the most expensive streets in the city. He parked at the end of the street, in front of a low concrete wall. A ladder was attached to the concrete wall, similar to ones used in public swimming pools, and Ollie realised that it was an easy way to get to the beach below the wall. In front of her was what she thought was the Øresund Strait, also known as The Sound, separating the city from the Swedish town of Malmo. It looked like a bolt of crushed, aqua velvet, embellished with Swarovski crystals. It was completely amazing.

Her new boss lived on the water... *Awesome.*

Ollie left the car and turned to look at the house on the right. The extensive property was clad in pale-pink-tinged timber, and sported multiple pitched roofs at different heights angled in different directions. It looked huge, which wasn't unexpected. Any man who could afford to pay her double her normal rate had deep pockets, so she'd expected a large, expensive house. But she hadn't expected such an interesting one and she couldn't wait to get inside.

Spending the summer here was not going to be a hardship in any way. The trees seemed greener, the flowers brighter and the air softer, as if nature was saying thank you for the break from the cold winter. She was looking forward to exploring this city, and hopefully she'd get a chance to see a bit more of the country while she was here. Because, frankly, anything was better than being in London and arguing with her family about her future with Cooper & Co.

Ollie, wearing her uniform of practical beige-coloured trousers and a white, men's-style button-down shirt, knocked on the black front door. She wore trendy trainers on her feet—high heels and little kids did not work well—and her corkscrew curls were pulled back by a plain black headband.

She was here for a job interview, not to compete in a 'model of the year' contest. Ollie felt a little nervous at hearing the sound of heavy footsteps behind the front door. She pulled a smile onto her face—just a small one; there was no need to look like an over-enthusiastic clown—and rubbed a suddenly damp hand on the seat of her trousers.

The door opened and Ollie's heart wasn't quite sure what to do with itself. On one hand, it wanted to do an over-excited backflip—if this was Bo Sø-renson, then he was hot! But if it *was* her new boss, the one she would be sharing a house with, then it wanted to do a failed bungee jump and splatter on the floor. Because, it meant he was her new boss and he was, well, hot.

Argh!

Ollie's heart thump-thumped as she took him in. He was a classic Nordic blond, tall and built, but not as pretty as some of the handsome Danish men she'd passed on her brief tour through the city. He was more rugged, a great deal more masculine. And his eyes weren't blue, they were a deep, mysterious green, the green of ancient woods and rain-splattered moss. She approved of the strong jawline under three-day stubble, his straight nose and what could be a sensual mouth. He was also bigger and taller than a lot of the other Danish men she'd seen, with wide shoulders and muscled legs. The bottom line was that he was panty-melting hot and wholly alpha, from his nicely shaped head to his rather big feet. Oh, he was alpha...so alpha.

And, damn it, Bo Sørenson had one of the best bodies she'd ever seen. And she very much wanted to see it naked.

Oh...oh, not good. So not good. Bad—as in, terrible. Sleeping with her boss would be not only supremely unprofessional, but also misconduct for which she could be fired. It was shocking to realise that it was a risk she would be willing to take. And this was, after all, her last job as a nanny...

Really—she was going there, five minutes after first laying eyes on him?

'Olivia Cooper?'

Ollie gave herself a mental slap and lifted her hand to shake the huge paw he held out. He gripped it, scowled at her and told her she was late. Ollie looked at her watch. It was only a couple of minutes past eleven, the time she said she would arrive at his house. Right, he was picky—sexy but rude.

Wonderful.

'I'm barely late, Mr Sørenson, so let's not start this interview by you splitting hairs,' Ollie told him coolly, brushing past him to step into his light-filled hall. She looked into the living area and sighed at the cool white-and-pale-blue walls, the sleek lines of designer furniture and the abundance of natural light. The lounge area, with huge windows that looked out onto the sea, had extra-high ceilings and, under the next ceiling with its lower and differently angled roof, was the kitchen and dining area. The two areas were separated by a glass-covered courtyard. It was very different, very lovely and very Scandinavian.

Ollie placed her bag on a chair in the hallway and folded her hands, tipping her head up, and up, to look into Bo Sørenson's scowling face. If he lost the fierceness, he would be an exceptional-looking man. Right now, he simply looked like an annoyed Viking.

Wonderful; she was being interviewed by Erik the Grouch.

'I'm pedantic about punctuality, Ms Cooper,' he stated.

But she hadn't been late!

'How was your trip, Ms Cooper? Did the driver find the house all right?' she returned, lifting her eyebrows. He needed her more than she needed him, she reminded herself. She'd been paid by her last family: this would be a bonus job. And, if she didn't get it, Goa was always an option if she couldn't bring herself to return to London before she was due—and she couldn't.

'Would you like a cup of coffee, now that you are *finally* here?'

Bo shoved his hands into the pockets of his casual trousers and pulled in a deep breath, then another. He had dark circles under his eyes, from lack of sleep or stress, and a muscle jumped in his jaw. Maybe her sarcasm was out of line, but she wasn't a fan of a lack of manners, and being snapped at before she'd had the chance to say hello. Nor was she a fan of feeling sexually sideswiped, desperate to slap her mouth on his, needing to discover whether he tasted as fine as he looked.

Bo shoved a hand into his short curls. His hair was the perfect shade of light caramel and the thick stubble on his face was several shades lighter. His nose was long and straight but that strong chin suggested stubbornness and pugnaciousness.

When he said nothing, and simply stood there taking her in, his face utterly expressionless, Ollie sighed. Right, it would be up to her to restart this conversation. 'Shall we start again? I'm Ollie Cooper and I've come to interview about the live-in nanny position.'

If he said something sarcastic, she would be out of there. 'Bo Sørenson,' he muttered, in a water-over-gravel voice. His English was almost perfect, with barely a trace of an accent. 'How was your trip? Would you like some coffee?'

Oh, she *knew* he was being sarcastic, but he'd asked the questions in such a bland voice that she couldn't call him out. Ollie pulled up a fake smile and thanked him. 'Fine. And, yes—black, two sugars.'

Bo nodded toward the living room and Ollie took that to mean that she should wait for him there while he made their coffee. She went through and walked to the left side of the room, where she knew she would be out of his sight, and gently bashed her head on the pale grey wall. Why oh, why, did her potential boss have to look like he was a chieftain in *Vikings*? Oh, he didn't have the long hair or the tattoos—not that she could see, anyway—but he had that Ragnar vibe that men listened to and made women melt. His energy filled a room; he was the type of guy people noticed…and women lusted over.

No, no, no!

Ollie rested her forehead against the cool wall and told herself to pull herself together immediately! Yes, he was a good-looking man—fantastically hot—but she was here to do a job, not drool over the man who was going to pay her a vast amount of money to look after his son. She was a professional—she prided herself on her detachment, her ability to be a part of the family but not intrude—but she'd never felt so overwhelmed by a man before. It made her jumpy, scatty and sarcastic, none of which were good traits when she was trying to land a job.

You either get this job or you go back to London. You either control your raging hormones or you move back into your childhood bedroom, still decorated with butterflies. You pull yourself together or you will find yourself in an office in Cooper & Co a lot sooner than you'd like. What are you going to choose, Olivia?

CHAPTER THREE

IN HIS KITCHEN, Bo carefully closed the door and rubbed his hands up and down his face, wondering if he'd stepped into a vortex that had tossed him arse-over-elbow and scrambled his brain.

On hearing the car pull up, he'd stood up and walked to the front door, expecting to see a middle-aged, slightly frumpy, stocky woman standing on his porch, a not-quite-so-terrifying version of Nanny McPhee—not an upgraded, sexy and updated version of Mary Poppins.

All the blood had rushed from his head as he'd taken in her fine-featured face, luminous brown eyes that turned upward at the corners, high cheekbones and her luscious, unblemished and creamy light-brown skin. Her corkscrew curls fell down her back and were held back from that far too gorgeous face by a plain black headband. She wore no make-up, from what he could see—she didn't need any—and was dressed in casual and contemporary trousers and a shirt. The body under that shirt had a small waist and long legs…and, yes, he'd noticed her breasts, round and high. He hadn't lingered on them—he wasn't a Neanderthal—but he was also a guy who liked women and he hadn't been able to help but notice.

She looked amazing.

This couldn't be happening to him—where was the stodgy, solid nanny he'd been expecting? The woman standing in his living room, probably wondering how long it took to make coffee, was reputedly one of the most sought-after nannies on the continent, spoken of in glowing terms by everyone who'd employed her. He'd read through her references carefully and recognised the names of some of the people she'd worked for, people of consequence and power. According to her references, she was punctual, honest, warm, kind and fantastic with children. Her former employers couldn't praise her enough and many stated they'd have her back in a heartbeat and that she would be a part of their lives for ever.

Well, he had told the owner of the agency he wanted the best, and it looked as though she'd delivered. But did the best have to come in such a drop-him-to-his-knees package? Olivia crackled with energy, and he loved her posh English accent and the unmistakable intelligence he saw in her eyes. Why was an accounting graduate working as a nanny? Where was her family? Did she have a lover?

Why was he so curious? He generally never asked these sorts of questions; he didn't have the time, energy or interest in small talk. But he wanted to know everything about Olivia—and immediately.

Bo sighed and wished he could put her on a plane and send her away, but he knew that finding another nanny so late in the day would be difficult—people would have made plans long before this, and finding someone as good as Olivia Cooper would be impossible. He would simply have to deal with his raging attraction to her and that would mean being even more imperturbable than he normally was. It was a good thing that he had so much practice hiding and dismissing his feelings. He'd need it today and over the next few months.

Right, get on with it, then, Sørenson.

Bo finished preparing the coffee. When he carried the tray into the room, he saw Olivia sitting on the edge of his couch, and noticed her looking as if she was about to jump out of her skin. So, he wasn't the only one feeling unbalanced. Good to know.

But there was no ignoring the fact that working and living with her was going to be a royal pain if they both couldn't relax. And that meant that he had to make an effort to make her feel welcome, to take the wariness out of her eyes.

The best way to do that was to address the elephant in the room and kick it out. 'I wasn't expecting an attractive young woman to be my new nanny.'

'Don't tell me, you were hoping for someone dressed like a bag lady with warts on her nose?' Olivia replied. 'Sorry to disappoint.'

The last thing Olivia could be called was disappointing. 'I reacted badly, and I was rude—I apologise. It's been a rough few days. But, before we go any further with this interview, we need to address the issue of me being a single father and you coming to live with a stranger.'

She hadn't expected him to be so upfront and surprise jumped into her very expressive eyes. She crossed her legs, leaned her forearm on her knee and held his gaze. 'Can I expect any trouble from you?'

Judging by her wary expression, she'd encountered that sort of trouble before. Men could be such morons.

'If by "trouble" you mean am I going to hit on you, then no. I have a very strict hands-off policy when it comes to my staff. I do not believe in making my life more complicated than it needs to be. You will be completely safe with me, Ms Cooper.'

Was that a flash of disappointment he caught in her eyes? No, it couldn't possibly be. He knew his imagination was playing tricks on him when her shoulders dropped and she leaned back slightly. Her actions told him that she wasn't attracted to him, and that she believed his reassurances. She should. Now that his words were out there, they couldn't be taken back. Unlike his father, Bo lived and died by his word. Once something was said, it was cast in stone.

Pity because, in any other situation, he would not have minded getting to know Olivia Cooper better. A lot better—naked better.

Yeah, not helpful, Sørenson.

'Thank you for that,' Olivia quietly stated. 'I appreciate you saying it.'

'But do you believe it?' It was important to Bo that if she took the job she felt safe here with him. He couldn't bear the thought of her tiptoeing around him on eggshells.

She held his eyes for a minute, as if looking for signs of deceit, and when she finally nodded he had to stop himself from sagging with relief. 'Yes, I do.'

Olivia nodded to the coffee on the table between them. 'Would you mind if I poured myself a cup? I'm gasping.'

'Absolutely.' Bo pushed the tray towards her and watched as her elegant fingers depressed the plunger, and then lifted the cafetière. Her nails were short and unvarnished, a pearly white against her skin. When she was done, he poured himself a cup, sat back and placed an ankle on the opposite knee. 'I've never interviewed a nanny before and, knowing nothing about children, I don't know what to ask you.'

She grinned and it was as if the sun had come out from behind a dark cloud. 'That's honest. So, why don't you tell me about your son and how he came to live with you? I understand it was...*unexpected*.'

'He's not here yet,' Bo informed her. He thought about how much to tell her and decided to give her the unvarnished truth.

Matheo's arrival in his life unexpected... 'Unexpected' was one word—'stunning' and 'world-changing' were others. 'I have never been shy about making my feelings about being in a committed relationship and having children known—I've never been interested in either and all my lovers knew where I stood. Somehow, despite my using condoms, Matheo's mother fell pregnant but she decided not to tell me. She returned to Brazil and she wanted to raise my son with the man she married after he was born. I am told he was going to adopt Matheo, but they both died in a car accident before that happened. Dani had put my name on the birth certificate and the authorities tracked me down and he's coming to live with me.'

He sipped at his coffee and tried and failed to smile. When he explained it out loud, it sounded even more outlandish than it did in his head. 'You're all up to date now, Olivia.'

'Call me Ollie,' she told him. 'That's an incredible story. So, where is Matheo now? Have you met him?'

Bo nodded, unable to explain his tumultuous day yesterday. He'd travelled to the house of Matheo's foster parents and, in their over-crowded living room, a homely woman had held a wide-eyed Matheo, his eyes big in his face. He'd been awake and had looked a little shell-shocked. Bo had wondered whether, on a visceral level, Matheo understood that his mum was gone. Their eyes had connected and a wave of love he'd never anticipated, hadn't expected or prepared for, had nearly dropped him to the floor.

This was his kid—*his*. His to raise, guide, protect and love. Look, he did not doubt that he could do the first three, but he was genuinely worried he couldn't give Matheo the love he needed. He'd never been shown how to love, how to nurture; he'd never been nurtured himself. But all he could do was his best, and he'd try.

Matheo had lunged forward and fallen into his arms, and he'd stood there for the longest time, feeling awkward as he held his son, trying to wrap his head around the fact that he was no longer alone and that he now had his own family. That, for the first time in his life, he'd fallen in love.

Bo looked at Ollie and tried to speak but found the words catching in his throat. Swallowing, he tried again. 'I met him yesterday. He's still at the foster mother's house; I am expecting him in an hour or so. The social worker wasn't convinced that I could look after him overnight without any help. I think she was worried that I'd lose him or forget about him or something. She wanted to wait until I had a nanny on the premises.'

Ollie tipped her head to the side. 'I think she was being overly protective. While you might be inexperienced, you would've muddled through, and Matheo would've been fine.'

He was surprised at the faith she showed in him. 'Why do you say that? I don't know anything about babies. Like, I know they cry and sleep, but that's about it.'

'You're not the first parent who would've had to learn on the job,' Ollie stated. She placed her cup on the tray and wrapped her hands around her knee. 'So, there are a few details we need to discuss. Can we do that?'

He liked her direct way of speaking, the way she looked him in the eye. He knew he could be intimidating but this woman, half his size, wasn't in the least bit afraid of him. That was a novelty, and he liked it. 'Sure.'

'You do realise that if I get the job I am only here for two months? I never take assignments that are longer than three months and the only reason I am here is because my other assignment was abruptly curtailed.'

He knew her sudden availability was due to her employer's change in plans, but he suspected there was a story behind that, and he wanted to know what it was.

No! He couldn't allow himself to become curious about his nanny, about what made her tick. At Sørenson Yachts, he kept his distance from his staff, but he might find that difficult to do with Ollie. Sure, his house was big—it had five bedrooms, each with its own *en suite*—but they were going to have to share the snug where he watched TV, this lounge and the kitchen and dining areas. If he hired her she would be employed to show him how to care for his son and that would mean they'd have to spend many hours together as he forged a bond with Matheo.

'The boss at the agency—Ms…' He frowned, not able to recall her name.

'Sabine du Foy,' Ollie interjected.

'Right, her—she made that clear. Apparently, you need to be back in London by the first of September.'

He saw her nose wrinkle just a little and wondered

why she wasn't keen on that. That she was English was obvious, but why wouldn't she want to go back to her home country?

Too many questions, Sørenson. Wrap your head around the concept of emotional distance, please. This has never been a problem for you before.

'I'll need a long-term nanny to take over from you. However, I'm not clear whether she will be looking for one for me, or whether you will take on that task.'

Ollie tapped her finger against her knee. 'We both will. Sabine will send me potential candidates and, if you are willing, I can pre-interview them for you. By that time, I will have a better understanding of your personality and needs, and I will make a short list for you. You can then interview the final candidates either by flying them to Copenhagen, as you've done for me, or via video call. I would suggest meeting them face to face.'

He did a lot of business over video but he far preferred to meet with someone one on one. With something as important as Matheo's safety, wellbeing and happiness at stake, he needed to look into someone's eyes, breathe the air they did and get a feel for them. He didn't want the barrier of a screen between them.

Ollie went on. 'I get a sense of someone's energy when I meet them face to face and I listen to my gut instincts.'

'What was your gut instinct reaction to me?' Bo asked, and nearly cursed aloud when the words left his mouth. What type of question was that, and how could he be so foolish to ask it?

Ollie tipped her head to the side, her gaze frank. 'I think you are take-no-prisoners direct, occasionally grumpy, ridiculously punctual—' he deserved that sarcastic aside '—and I suspect that you can, on occasion, be a considerable pain in the butt.'

Ollie smiled so sweetly that Bo couldn't help a small grin hitting his lips. 'Accurate.'

'I know.' Bo expected her to ask him what his first impressions of her had been—*sexy, gorgeous, confident and super smart*—but she didn't, and he liked that about her. She didn't seem to need his approval; she was immensely comfortable in her skin and in her abilities to do the job she'd applied for. Confidence was such a turn-on.

'So, are we going to do this, Mr Sørenson? Are you going to let me look after your son for the next eight weeks?'

Of course he was. He was sure she was the best there was. He nodded.

Ollie leaned back in her chair, a contented smile on her face. 'It's good to know that the flight wasn't wasted,' she said. 'Now, why don't you tell me about your working day, so that I know your routine?'

He rose early, hit the gym and was in his office before seven. He frequently didn't come home until after nine or ten. He seldom broke for lunch, drank pre-made smoothies for breakfast and picked up pre-pared meals for supper. If he kept up that schedule, he'd never see Matheo. But if he didn't work this summer, he'd never manage to hit his clients' dead-lines. *Damn it.*

'Can I get back to you on that?' he asked Ollie. 'And, if I get to call you Ollie, then you must call me Bo.'

'Bo. So, get back to me on your schedule and we'll work something out.' She turned and cocked her head; Bo also heard the car pulling into his drive-way. He shot to his feet and pushed a hand into his hair.

'Uh, that will be Matheo…'

Ollie was also on her feet but, in contrast to him, she looked completely calm. How could she be so calm? His life was taking a one-eighty spin; every-one should be as freaked out as he was. Ollie placed a hand on his bare forearm and her touch calmed his racing heart, allowing him to pull some air into his lungs. 'I'm here, Bo, and I'm here to help. Just take a couple of deep breaths, okay?'

She made it sound as if he was panicking and he never panicked. He'd sailed catamarans in the Bering Sea, had done the occasional free climb and had base-jumped before. He was the calmest per-son he knew. He knew how to regulate his breath-ing, to calm his nerves. He didn't let emotion affect him. He could, more often than not, be a robot in human form.

But, at this moment, his brain wanted to jump out of his skull and his heart was squeezing through a gap in his ribs. He was taking on a child, another human being. He was going to be *responsible* for a baby human—from this moment, Matheo's growth, mental, emotional and physical, would all be on him. He'd never wanted this and at that moment, consumed by terror, he hated Dani for dying and leaving him to raise a child he'd never wanted.

He dropped to his haunches and rested his fingertips on the floor to balance himself. Then he felt a small hand on his shoulder, a gentle '*you've got this*' squeeze, and a little air slid into his lungs. He wasn't alone, he wasn't doing this by himself. For the next two months or so, he'd have Ollie's help, her experienced, knowledgeable, studied help. She was his two-month back-up plan, a way to get him up to speed.

This situation was not Matheo's fault, and neither was it his—it just was what it was. And he could either sit here, imitating a rather wobbly jelly, or he could stand up, square his shoulders, open that door and face the future.

He could do this. Because he had no damn choice.

Bo stood up, walked to the hallway and placed his hand on the door, closing his eyes as he gathered his courage to open it. He was stepping out of his solo world and becoming a family... Man, he was terrified. But courage, as they said, was doing something whether you were scared or not.

He yanked the door open so hard that it bounced back and he had to step away so it didn't smack him in the face. Catching the frame, he eased the door out of his way and looked at Mrs Daniels with Matheo perched on her hip. His son was awake but

Bo could see the streaks of dried tears on his face. And maybe he was projecting here, but in his green eyes he saw all his fear.

Matheo shoved a thumb into his mouth. Bo didn't pull his eyes off him and ran his knuckle down his smooth cheek. 'Have you had a rough day, little man?'

Surprising him, Matheo, leaned towards him and Mrs Daniels handed him over. Matheo immediately curled himself into Bo's chest, resting his head against it. Through his thin shirt, Bo could feel the rhythmic beat of his little heart. Bo covered Matheo's head with his big hand and, ignoring Mrs Daniels, dropped a kiss in his hair. 'It's okay, Mat, you're home. I've got you.'

Matheo looked up at him, blinked once and sent Bo the sweetest smile, revealing one little tooth. And Bo, hard and short-tempered, realised that his heart—that misshapen, mangled organ that's sole purpose was to pump blood around his body—no longer belonged to him.

CHAPTER FOUR

THE SOCIAL WORKER arrived with not much more than a few clothes, a couple of nappies and a yellow, ratty dog that Matheo couldn't seem to live without. On doing a quick inspection of Bo's house, Ollie realised he didn't have anything they'd need for the child. They wouldn't last the night.

What had he been thinking—that Matheo would move in and eat adult food and drink whiskey? Where was the baby going to sleep; what was he going to eat, wear? Ollie understood that acquiring a baby had been a shock but Bo—obviously intelligent—was either clueless, still in shock or maybe a little of both.

To be fair, she wasn't at her best either. Not only was she dreading the future, but this job would go by super-quickly, and she was also feeling way off-balance. Her new, single boss was the sexual equivalent of an asteroid strike and she felt as if she was a tiny star he'd bumped off course and was now spinning around in space.

She'd never had such an intense reaction to a

man before: she was far too sensible and practical to be blown out of her sexual boots. Her ex had been a good choice, a sensible choice and, had he not cheated on her and been so unsympathetic about Becca—she'd been more upset by the second than the first—she'd still be with him. He'd been a reasonable and safe option, someone her family had liked: good-looking enough, with a good job and a good conversationalist. A steady, not too shiny star.

Bo was a meteorite, a shooting star and a black hole—mysterious, foreign, unexplained, interesting and utterly fascinating.

And, as he'd taken care to explain earlier, very off-limits. She had to stop thinking about him as a sexy man she'd like to kiss and get it into her head that he was her boss. And that meant sorting out this rag-tag, thrown-together family.

Because it was her job, Ollie immediately sprang into action. When Matheo—henceforth to be known as the cutest kid in the world and a Bo mini-me—fell asleep in the middle of Bo's huge California King bed, surrounded by cushions higher than the Great Wall of China, Ollie sat down at the rustic table in Bo's gourmet kitchen and started making a list.

She looked up as Bo entered the kitchen, having changed into a smarter shirt and pulled a pair of loafers over his sockless feet. He held his car keys in his hand and his hair was brushed. Ollie leaned back in her chair and gave him a long up-and-down look.

'I'm going to go to work for a few hours—I need to get some things done.'

Nope. Not going to happen. Ollie draped her arm over the back of the chair and shook her head. 'No, you're not.'

His deep-green gaze turned cold. 'I'm sorry, I thought I heard you trying to tell me what to do. In case this arrangement wasn't clear, I tell you what to do.'

Ollie didn't have time to deal with his lord of the manor routine right now. 'So tell me, *Mr Søren-son*—' she put extra emphasis on the word '—where is Mat going to sleep tonight? In your bed with you? I don't recommend that. How is he going to eat—off a lap or in a chair? You can't bathe him with your expensive, top-of-the-range products, he needs toi-letries suitable for a baby. You're running low on nappies and there is no baby formula, so what do you intend to feed him? I'm not going to run out at midnight in a city I don't know looking for emer-gency supplies.'

His eyes bounced from her face to the list on the table in front of her. His shoulders slumped. 'I… eh…didn't think.'

Well, that much was obvious.

'What did you think? That he was just going to fall asleep and then wake up when you were done with your work?' Ollie asked, trying not to roll her eyes. When Bo frowned, she knew she hadn't been successful in hiding her impatience.

'Okay, clever clogs, I get your point.'

'We need supplies, and we need them fast.'

He gestured to a closed laptop sitting on the dining table. 'You can use that. It runs everything in the house. You can order whatever you need and they'll deliver.'

Ollie shook her head. 'I think I need to go myself. I saw a speciality baby shop not far from here. It will have everything I need.' She saw the confusion in his eyes and knew that he'd never noticed the impressive-looking baby shop just a few blocks away. Why should he? Babies hadn't been his thing up until the day before yesterday.

The man was going to have a big wake-up call.

'If you can stay here and look after Mat, I'll drive down to the store and get everything I need. Also, walking around the store will jolt my memory— there will be things we'll need that I've forgotten. It's been a while since I looked after a baby.'

Bo ran a hand through his hair in frustration. 'I've just got him and you want to leave me alone with him?' he demanded, fear jumping into his eyes.

'He's probably going to sleep for a couple of hours and I should be back by then,' Ollie told him.

Bo shook his head, dug into his back pocket and pulled out a slim-line wallet. He flipped it open, removed a black credit card, handed it over and told her the pin. 'Buy whatever you need but be quick about it. I'll go to work when you get back.'

Seriously? Again, no.

Ollie felt another spurt of annoyance but it died when she saw the confusion and fear in his eyes. He was very out of his depth and floundering. He needed to feel in control and he could do that at work, the place where everything made complete sense and there were few surprises. But running off would just delay the inevitable and, the sooner he and Matheo settled into their new reality, the better they'd all be.

'I'm going to have to order a load of stuff to be delivered here. When I get back, I will need help assembling it—Mat's cot, putting his feeding chair together and maybe even assembling his changing station. I cannot do all of that and look after a baby. And I thought you wanted to learn how to look after him?'

'I do, but—'

'But?'

He glanced away. 'But I also need to work.'

The quicker he learned that he had to fit into Matheo's timetable, and not the demands of the company, the easier this process would be. At least until they established some routine and found some long-term help.

'I think you should consider putting work onto the back burner for the next little while—or, if you must work, do it when Mat goes down for the night. He needs to get used to you and to start recognising you as his primary care-giver, the one stable person in his life. He's not going to be able to do that if you keep flitting off to work.'

Bo opened his mouth to argue and Ollie lifted her eyebrows, waiting for his response. He was looking for an out clause, a way to make this work for him, but in the end couldn't come up with one. This was his new reality and it was smacking him in the face.

Ollie picked up the list and tucked it in the back pocket of her trousers with his credit card. 'I need a car.'

Bo nodded to a lovely pottery bowl on the dining table, in swirls of rich blues and green, within which lay a keyless fob. 'I suppose you'll have to take my car. Can you drive a manual? Are you used to power? Maybe I should go grab what's needed and you should stay here.'

He was grabbing at the last straw, still trying to run, but she wouldn't let him. She shook her head. 'Bo, I have driven a variety of expensive cars and, yes, I can drive a manual car. What is it?'

'It's a two-seater Mercedes GLS,' Bo told her. Right, it was only a rare, pricey car—she'd better not ding it. It was also hugely impractical for a man with a baby.

'Where are you going to put a baby seat in that?' Ollie asked him. 'On the roof? Maybe, while I'm gone, you could consider doing some car shopping, unless you never intend to take Mat anywhere.'

Ollie scooped up the fob and walked out of the kitchen and down the passage. Matheo hadn't moved from his position within the pillows. She returned to the kitchen where Bo still stood, looking a little shell-shocked. She placed her hand on his muscled, warm forearm and looked up into his hunky face. 'Bo, you need to keep checking on Mat—like, every ten minutes. You do not want him falling off the bed.'

He nodded. 'I'll take my laptop into the bedroom and work from there.'

Right, he hadn't got the message. He rolled his eyes at her disbelief. 'I was going to research which cars are the safest children-carriers and then I was going to call my car guy.'

Ah. Right. She'd made an assumption and it was way off the mark. It wouldn't pay to underestimate Bo Sørenson. He might not say a lot but he heard a great deal.

It was past nine when Bo finally sat down with a glass of wine. He slumped down onto his white couch and propped his bare feet up onto the coffee table. He was categorically exhausted. His first Mat-centric day had wiped him out. For a guy who regularly ran half-marathons, who spent hours in the gym and who was known for being able to work sixteen-hour days without breaking a sweat, he could not believe that a twenty-pound child had made him want to sleep for a week.

And it wasn't as if he'd had to do that much. A few minutes after Ollie had swung back into his driveway and parked his precious car, a delivery van had pulled up and started unloading what looked to be half a house. The men were dressed in smart overalls bearing the logo of the shop where she'd spent the equivalent of a small country's health budget—he'd got a notification from the bank when she'd swiped his card, convinced the comma was in the wrong place. The men hauled the furniture out of the van and carried it into the room they'd designated should be Mat's. They'd then hauled out screwdrivers and

Allen keys and had swiftly built the furniture she'd bought, including a wooden feeding chair and a cabinet for the pile of clothes she'd purchased.

A cot with sides that dropped down was pushed into the corner of the room and a colourful mobile was attached to the side. Toiletries were placed in the *en suite* bathroom and Ollie, who'd turned into a whirling dervish of activity, tossed his new clothes into the washer/dryer. She had also purchased a range of organic baby food, telling him that it would do for now, but she'd teach him how to make Mat's food herself.

He didn't even cook for himself and she expected him to cook for his son?

While all this was going on, Ollie taught him how to change a nappy, how to bathe a wriggling Mat and made him hold and walk him while he yelled his head off for who knew what. Ollie had told him that he was just feeling unsettled and a little scared, and that he had to remain calm, that babies were amazingly good at picking up on emotions. Bo had tried but, judging by how long it had taken Mat to stop crying, he knew he needed better relaxation techniques.

He took a huge sip of wine and looked at the baby monitor on the coffee table. He could hear Mat's soft breathing and he closed his eyes and inhaled. He had a child…in his house. And would be sharing his space for at least the next eighteen to twenty years…

A couple of days ago he'd been responsible for no one but himself, and today he was raising a child. Bo sat up, placed his forearms on his knees and tried to keep the ribbons of terror threatening to wrap him up in knots. He couldn't do this, he didn't know how to…

'Are you okay there? You're looking a little green.'

Bo looked up to see Ollie standing in the doorway to the living room, her face still looking as fresh as it had when she'd first arrived this morning. Her white shirt looked a little wilted, her trousers had a streak of something on her thigh and she'd lost her hairband, so her curls fell in disarray down the sides of her heart-shaped face, but he could feel waves of energy rolling off her. He had all the energy of a wet noodle but he suspected she could carry on for a few more hours. All he wanted was his bed—and, preferably, Ollie in it.

Was he just reacting to her like this because his life had been turned inside out and because, at times like these, it was natural to look for help, for someone to share the load of what was honestly an overwhelming experience? Was he just experiencing a millennia-old biological urge?

There's a woman, she knows what she's doing, I'll have her.

He was too honest with himself, about himself, to use that handy excuse for his prickly skin, the movement in his trousers or the hitch of his breath. The inconvenient truth was that Ollie would have caught his eye and interest no matter where or when he'd met her. There was something about her that made him look, look again and wonder.

She wasn't cover-girl pretty—he'd had lovers who'd strutted the catwalks of Milan and Paris—but his eyes were constantly drawn back to her face. He liked eyes upturned at the corners, her wide smile and the hint of a dimple in her left cheek. She was a combination of sexy and sensible, practical and pretty. Ollie was efficient and unflappable and he wouldn't have coped today—*had he coped?*—without her calm attitude, flashes of sly humour and pragmatism.

Bo ran his hand down his face; an employee living with him was not a good idea. He gestured to his wine glass. 'Would you like a glass?'

Ollie wrinkled her nose. 'I shouldn't.'

Bo knew she was thinking about whether it was professional or not to have a glass of wine with her employer. 'Ollie, you've had a long, long day. Mat is asleep. Have a glass of wine and wind down.'

She stepped into the room and nodded her thanks. Bo headed for the kitchen, found another glass, poured her some wine and handed it over. Ollie immediately kicked off her shoes and curled up in his favourite chair, her feet tucked under her bottom and her head resting against the soft leather. She sipped and sighed. Bo resumed his seat on the leather couch and stretched out his long legs, placing his hand over his mouth to cover a yawn. 'How can I be so tired?' he asked.

'It's been a life-changing day for you, and emotional tiredness is a lot more sapping than physical tiredness,' Ollie told him, and there was a depth of authenticity in her voice that made Bo suspect that she knew of what she spoke. She met his eyes, lifted her glass in a toast and handed him a soft smile. 'Congratulations on your new kid, Bo. He's a cracker.'

A wave of pride washed over him and he smiled. 'He really is,' he admitted. 'But, man, I didn't realise how much work babies involved.'

'Today was an extraordinary day. Once you are in a routine and know what you're doing, it'll get easier and will come more naturally to you.'

He so didn't know what he was doing. He hoped she was right. If not, he was going to spend the next twenty years running around like a headless chicken. For someone who loved control and order, a man who enjoyed being successful and knowledgeable, it was a terrifying thought. He looked over to Ollie and took in her shocking-pink toenails, the ring on her middle toe, and her soft-looking, elegant feet. He had a hot, smart woman sitting in his living room and he was not only exhausted but they'd only discussed babies. A day or two ago, he'd been an in-demand yacht designer, melded to his work. Today he was a dad.

He rested the foot of his glass on one knee. 'I never really interviewed you this morning,' he said, thinking back on the day.

Ollie raised her eyebrows. 'Are you telling me you are still deciding whether to hire me?'

Bo thought he heard a hint of tease in her voice but he was so out of the practice with being teased—if he ever had been—that he couldn't be sure. 'No, of course not—you're hired.'

He caught the twitch of her lips and knew that he'd been had. It was so strange that this pint-sized person wasn't in the least bit wary of his bark—compared to his six-four height and big build, she was a feather. 'Does anyone intimidate you?'

She considered his question, her hair dropping way past her shoulder as she tipped her head to the side. 'Honestly? My mum.'

Ollie waved her hand in the general direction of the bedrooms. 'Take my organisational skills today and multiply them by a thousand and you'll get my mum. She worked full-time as a chartered accountant, raised four boys and a girl and still managed to be a very hands-on mum. God help the world if my mum decides to ever take it in hand.'

That Ollie loved her mum was obvious, but there was a note of wistful defiance in her voice, something that suggested that she and her mum bumped heads on occasion. Choosing not to pry, as he hated it when people dug into his family situation, he asked another question. 'You have *four* brothers?'

Ollie took another sip of her wine and nodded. 'Four older, very bossy, very protective brothers. I'm the youngest.'

Ah. With four brothers and a strong mum, it was no wonder that he didn't intimidate her. Actually, it was quite nice. Having people tiptoe around him was sometimes annoying, mostly unnecessary and always frustrating. Yeah, he was big, and he had a serious face, but he didn't routinely bite people's heads off. He demanded a certain standard from his employees, and made it known if he wasn't happy with their performance, but he didn't play games and he never held grudges.

'I'm starving,' Bo realised, looking towards the kitchen and then at his watch. It was past nine, he didn't have the energy to cook and the last thing he wanted to do was go out to eat. *Oh, wait, I can't do that any more.*

Ollie looked at her watch and smiled. 'I ordered two pizzas—one fully loaded, one a plain Margherita. They should be here in about ten minutes.'

Ah...what? Ollie smiled at his confusion. 'When you were trying to dry and dress Mat—not very successfully—I realised that neither of us would have the time to cook tonight. I was starving, and I presumed you would be too, so I ordered pizza. I thought it was the easiest option because everyone eats pizza.'

He was impressed by her ability to think ahead but couldn't resist trying his hand at teasing. 'I could be gluten-intolerant.'

Ollie started to roll her eyes and then seemed to remember that he was her boss and stopped. Yep, his new nanny was not going to be deferential or demure. He genuinely couldn't be more thrilled about that. 'I saw you stuffing a biscuit into your mouth earlier, so I figured you weren't.'

'Smart arse,' he grumbled, but his small smile told

her that he was amused. And she did amuse him. When had a woman last done that? He couldn't remember.

Hoping that the pizza would arrive soon, he walked over to the kitchen area and picked up the bottle of wine standing on the marble island. He nodded to her half-empty glass. 'Can I give you more?'

Ollie clutched the glass to her chest and shook her head, causing her curls to bounce. 'I'm a lightweight with alcohol. One glass is my limit, and I probably won't even finish that.'

Bo topped up his own glass, walked over to the window and looked out onto the fantastic view of the Øresund Strait. He opened the bi-fold doors and sucked up in a dose of fresh, warm air. He watched the lights of a boat, maybe a trawling vessel, making its way up the straight and asked Ollie another question. 'How did you become a nanny? I think I remember seeing something about you having an accounting degree. Quite a good one, if I recall correctly.'

He turned round just in time to see a flash of distaste cross her face. 'Not a fan of figures?' he asked.

'I left university and, instead of joining the family's accounting business, I wanted to travel. I needed a way to support myself so I applied to an agency— Sabine du Foy's—and I looked after Sabine's sister's kids for a year or two. Sabine, as you can imagine, has connections all over Europe and I went to look after the children of another influential family. I've been doing this for five years, and have worked for a lot of families.'

'And were they all good?'

Ollie rocked her right hand. 'Mostly. Mostly they were fabulous, one or two were less than. It happens.'

He wondered which side of the scale he'd tip when she left. And that reminded him of something else. 'Ms du Foy said that I was lucky to get you and that you only work three-month contracts. Why? Why don't you stay longer?'

Those long legs unfurled and her feet hit the floor. Ollie stood up, her expression shuttered. Right, whatever ease they'd developed he'd blown up with his last question. It hadn't been highly personal, and one he should've asked earlier when interviewing her for the position. But, seeing her reaction, he could see it was a hot button for her. And he wanted to know why.

Ollie drained the last of her wine and, when her brown eyes met his, he couldn't see any of the flecks of gold he'd caught in them earlier. 'I don't stay longer because I won't allow myself to get attached.' She managed to smile but it was tight. 'I'm just going to wash my hands; by the time I get back the pizza should be here. If you don't mind, I'm going to have a quick slice and then go to bed. It's been a very long day.'

Bo watched her walk away, her spine straight and her rounded hips swaying. If he hadn't asked that last question, they would've shared the pizza, sitting on either side of the island, chatting amicably, getting to know each other.

But his curiosity had blown that possibility out of

the water. And maybe that wasn't a bad thing. She was his nanny, an employee, and he shouldn't be getting friendly with her.

Employee.

Hired to look after his son.

Then why couldn't he stop thinking about how her body must look under her clothes, whether her hair was as soft as it looked and whether her mouth was sexy or spicy?

Good job on making a complicated situation way more intricate than it needed to be, Sørenson.

CHAPTER FIVE

OLLIE, IN THE small garden outside the kitchen door, moved her body into a downward dog pose and turned her head to the right to look at Mat, who sat on a blanket she'd laid out on the grass, gnawing on a plastic teething toy she'd picked up yesterday. She'd heard him wake just before six. He'd slept through the night, the amazing child, and she'd gone to him, changing his nappy and giving him a 'good morning' cuddle. She'd warmed a bottle for him and he'd happily sucked the milk down. Since he'd looked happy enough, she plopped him down next to her and decided to try and get in a quick yoga routine.

Yoga and running kept her centred and supple, and calmed her constantly whirring mind. But this morning she was finding it difficult to clear her mind. She pulled in a deep breath and wished she'd handled Bo's question about why she only worked for three months at a time with more sangfroid. She'd answered the question many times before, blithely telling people that she was the bridge between their old nanny and their new. Bo was the first person whom she'd told, openly and honesty, that she didn't stick around because she was afraid of getting attached. She'd never voiced those words aloud before.

Memories, both sweet and sour, tumbled through her. She'd loved working for the De Freidmans. They'd been a perfect family—three kids under the age of ten, the mother a human rights lawyer, and the father a heart surgeon. The older boys had been mischievous but lovely, but it was four-year-old Rebecca who'd captured Ollie's heart. Serious and a little geeky, the little girl had asked profound questions, was a frequent hugger and was simply the nicest child she'd ever come across. Becca had loved everyone and everyone had loved her. Their house in Bruges had been lovely, and Ollie had been so happy with her converted attic apartment, the city and the friends she'd made there.

Then everything had changed when Ollie had suggested a check-up because she thought Becca was low on energy. The doctors had done myriad tests on her tiny body and Rebecca had been diagnosed with brain cancer. There had been no cure: if they were lucky, Becca had a year to live.

Although Ollie had been close to the family up until that point, she'd been accepted as part of it then, and she'd become Johannes's and Petra's strength and support. To them, she'd been the one person who understood, like no one else could, what the world would lose when Becca passed on. As Becca's illness progressed, Ollie's connection to the little girl, and the family, had grown stronger. Every day she'd fallen a little more in love as she'd stored up memories of the precious child she'd have so little time with.

For eight months the De Friedmans had become her world and their house was the only place she'd wanted to be. Calls to Fred, her fiancé, had stopped, his calls to her had gone unanswered and she'd rarely connected with her family. Fred, her family and Sabine had all warned her she was getting in too deep and that she was losing perspective but all she'd been able to think about that was that Becca was dying. She'd needed to spend as much time with her as she could, and had been driven to support the family through what was the worst situation any parents could find themselves in.

In hindsight, she'd lost herself for those eight months. Sabine had even flown to Bruges to talk to her, and she'd tried to get Ollie to take some time off, but Ollie had refused.

And then Rebecca had died and a little piece of Ollie died with her too. Just a week after the funeral, a conversation with Johannes and Petra had ripped her apart...

'Miss?'

Ollie looked up from her downward dog pose into a round, homely face dominated by the most amazing pair of blue eyes. She stood up, putting herself between Mat and this stranger. While she did not doubt that this lady was harmless, as she was in Bo's garden, she was still a stranger to Ollie.

'I was wondering if you'd like some breakfast, miss.'

Ollie folded her arms across her bare stomach—
she wore only a cropped exercise top and a brief
pair of cycling shorts. 'I'm sorry but who are you?'

'I'm Greta Jensen, Bo's housekeeper.' She
dropped to her haunches in front of Mat and smiled
at the baby boy. Mat's reciprocal smile was a great
deal more gummy and drooly. 'And this is little Mat.
Oh, he looks just like Bo.'

Right, so Bo had told his housekeeper that he had
a son, but he'd failed to inform Ollie that he had a
housekeeper. They were going to have to work on
their communication skills. And where was the man?
It was after seven; shouldn't he be up by now?

'I'm Ollie, Mat's nanny,' Ollie said, looking at her
yoga mat. She was only halfway through her routine
and she needed another twenty minutes to unwind
and work the knots out of her body.

Because she'd been thinking about Rebecca, Fred
and her family—focusing on past grief, hurt and her
current confusion—her mind would take a great deal
more time to unknot. She needed hours of stretching,
possibly days of meditation. It was time she didn't
have and, frankly, didn't want to spend.

It was easier to stay unattached and remaining
distant than work through emotional quagmires, another good reason to live her life solo. Why would
she want the insecurity associated with a boyfriend
or a lover? Who needed the 'does he love me?', 'is
this just about sex?', and 'will he still want me if I
pick up five kilograms and get a spot on my chin?'
questions? She was already dealing with one situa-

tion she wasn't keen on—the thought of working as an accountant—why would she want to deal with more than she needed to?

'Shall I take him inside with me?' Greta asked. 'I will put him in his new feeding chair. I see you put some porridge out for his breakfast. I can make that for him, if you'd like. He can keep me company while I make Bo's breakfast. I can make you some too.'

She'd been a nanny long enough to know that it was in her best interests to take any help when it was offered. And she could see Mat's high chair from here and would know within seconds if he got fretful or weepy. 'That sounds amazing, thank you.'

Greta scooped Mat up and placed him on her slim hip. It was obvious that she had experience with children. 'I raised four children and have six grandchildren,' Greta told her when Ollie asked.

Right. Why on earth had Bo employed her as a nanny when he had such an experienced woman working for him already? 'You should be Mat's nanny,' Ollie told her, keeping her tone light.

'I only work half-days for Bo a few times a week,' Greta explained. She sent Ollie a naughty smile. 'And, while I adore children, I very much like being able to give them back when I've had enough.'

Fair enough. Greta walked Mat into the kitchen and Ollie dropped back down to her mat, pushing her body into a cat cow. She'd continue with some basic moves for a few minutes before attempting the more complicated poses she'd spent a long time mastering.

Ollie was just getting into the zone, her mind reasonably still, when she heard the side gate open and slam close and rough breathing behind her. Dropping her foot, she whirled around to see Bo standing next to the gate, his attention on the smart watch on his wrist. He pushed buttons and nodded his satisfaction as Ollie stood there, staring at him.

That he was a big guy was obvious but, with him dressed in casual clothes yesterday, she hadn't quite realised how big he was, or how muscled. In his athletic shorts and low-hanging vest, she noticed that his arms were huge, his legs muscled and that big muscles covered the balls of his shoulders and above his collarbone. She knew, without a shadow of a doubt, that he'd have a washboard stomach and could see that his chest, sprinkled with a fine layer of blond-brown hair, was as defined. He was gorgeous. Hot, ripped...

So very off-limits.

'Morning,' she said, shocked to hear her voice sounding deeper than normal and a little sultry.

His eyes darted between her, the blanket on the grass and the teething ring Greta had left behind. 'Where's Mat?'

'Greta has him.'

Bo nodded. His eyes met hers and she was pulled into a glinting green fire as he took in what she was wearing. His eyes meandered down her body and over her breasts. Annoyingly, her nipples puckered, and his lips quirked. His gaze moved down her flat stomach and she felt the heat of his gaze on her legs, between her legs. She saw him swallow and watched as he pushed back his hair with one forearm.

His erection tented his shorts, and Ollie knew he liked what he saw. He was as attracted to her as she was to him. She'd been hoping that he'd be the one to keep the situation professional, their interactions on an even keel. She was wrong.

Damn this was not good. She really, really wanted to kiss him, to lay her hands on that big, masculine, oh-so-strong body. It had been a while, so she desperately wanted his arms around her, his mouth covering hers...

And the desire burning in his eyes told her he wanted that too.

'We shouldn't act on our mutual attraction...that would complicate matters.'

Ollie appreciated the fact that he could be honest about their attraction, that he didn't pussy-foot around and pretend it wasn't happening. She appreciated people being candid and preferred to look at situations as they were, not how she wanted them to be.

'I know,' she agreed, rubbing the back of her neck. 'I don't sleep with my employers.'

'And I don't sleep with my employees,' he countered.

Ollie nodded and folded her arms across her chest, locking them in tight so that she didn't throw herself at him. She didn't recognise herself: she'd never reacted so intensely, so quickly, to a man. She felt as if she was a piece of kindle soaked in petrol and he was an unexpected spark…

Together she was certain they could burn down Copenhagen.

Ollie watched as Bo pulled in some deep breaths, and she did the same. The crackle of electricity that arced between them faded to a low buzz and, now that she wasn't feeling overwhelmed by lust, Ollie could hear the sound of Greta talking to Mat, the sound of the washing machine churning and the little boy laughing.

She should be looking after Mat right now, making his breakfast and planning a new routine to make the baby feel more settled. She should not be out here, waiting and hoping to be kissed by her boss. Bo was paying her an extraordinary amount of money to give his son the best care she could, and she was doing yoga and dreaming of snogging his father.

She might be leaving the industry but she could leave with her head held high, knowing that she'd done the best she could. She shuffled down the wall and stepped away from Bo. 'If you'll excuse me, Mr Sørenson…'

'Look, Ollie, we don't need to be so formal.'

She gave him a tight smile. 'I really think we do. It might…' she hesitated, looking for the right word '…help.'

Ollie walked away from him, knowing that she did need to keep the formalities, and a considerable amount of personal space, between her and her employer. She didn't allow herself to have affairs with her employers and Bo would be no different.

Neither would she get attached. She'd look after Mat for two months and move on. Not staying still, not allowing roots to find any soil, was what she did best.

Two nights later, Bo walked Mat up and down the living room, jiggling his sobbing son in his arms. It was Ollie's night off, he was on Mat duty and he couldn't get his son to stop crying. He'd changed his nappy, given him a bottle and rocked him incessantly but Mat had yet to stop howling. Bo thought that there was a good possibility that he would cave and start crying soon too. It was three-forty in the morning and he'd had about an hour's sleep. He had a client meeting in the morning to talk over the changes he'd made to his racing yacht and, thanks to Mat falling into his life, he hadn't done enough preparation. It was going to be a disaster but, right now, Bo was too tired to care.

He'd heard that having a kid was hard, but this was beyond ridiculous. How did parents do this day in and day out without going off their heads? He missed his life, he missed his sleep, he missed work and he missed making decisions without having to think about how they affected anyone else.

Bo looked down into his little boy's miserable face and guilt rushed through him, as cold as a melting glacier. His parents had resented him; they'd never admitted it but, even with the help of au pairs and nannies, he'd seriously cramped their style. He'd felt as if he was a burden, a hanger-on, standing outside the circle of their lives.

He'd never make his child feel anything but loved. And if that meant sacrificing some sleep, not being at his best at a client meeting or delegating some responsibility at work, that was what he'd do. He could be a dad. He *was* a dad. This was his life now.

His life had flipped over and inside out, but becoming a single father was as far as he would go. Despite coming close to kissing Ollie the other day, nothing would, or could, happen between them. She wasn't going to morph from being a nanny to being Mat's mummy: she was a short-term solution, not a long-term fixture. He'd paid for her help but he couldn't allow any woman into his life on a long-term basis; he couldn't trust anyone with that much of himself. He couldn't allow his feelings to take over, to crack open his hard carapace.

He'd wanted to be loved once and, when that love had never come, he'd vowed he'd never seek it again. Rejection hurt, and not being loved enough, or at all, would rip his soul apart. He'd avoid that, thank you very much.

'Please stop crying, Mat,' Bo whispered, his lips on Mat's blond hair. 'I beg of you, just please stop.'

Bo moved Mat up onto his shoulder and held him under his butt, his big hand almost covering Mat's back, which he gently patted. Mat snuffled, yawned and Bo held his breath. Was this it? Was he finally going to go to sleep? He'd do anything…

'Waah...!'

Bo walked over to the nearest wall and banged his forehead against it.

'No luck, huh?'

Bo turned to see Ollie standing in the doorway to the hall, her light cotton dressing-gown open over a vest top and a small pair of sleeping shorts. She was barefoot and he caught the shimmer of the fine silver ankle chain she wore around her left ankle. Her hair was all over the place and there was a pillow crease on her left cheek.

'Sorry, I thought this house was big enough that his crying wouldn't wake you up,' Bo said as she walked across the room to where he stood. Bo caught a whiff of citrus, wondered whether it was her soap or shampoo and told himself to concentrate.

Ollie placed the back of her hand on Bo's forehead and shook her head. 'He doesn't have a temperature,' she observed, her hand on Mat's back. 'I don't think he's sick.'

'Then why won't he stop crying?' Bo demanded, feeling as though he was hanging onto the last strand of a very frayed rope.

'He's teething,' Ollie told him. She slipped her finger into Mat's mouth and, surprisingly, Mat let her. When she removed it, she nodded. 'Yep, his gum is swollen.'

Right. Teething was the last thing he would've checked for.

'We can give him a spoonful of a mild, perfectly

harmless painkiller, if you feel comfortable doing that,' Ollie suggested.

'You bought him medicine?' Bo asked, following Ollie as she walked back to Mat's nursery.

In the shadows of the dark nursery, he saw the flash of white teeth and the gleam in her eye. 'I bought him *everything*. Didn't you see how much I spent?' Ollie asked as they moved further into the room.

He had and he didn't much care. He had money and, right now, if it meant Mat getting some sleep, and him getting some too, he'd pay anything he needed to. Ollie walked into the bathroom attached to Mat's room and Bo heard the cabinet opening and closing. She returned with a tiny syringe filled with liquid and placed it in Mat's mouth, depressing the plunger.

'It should work fairly quickly,' Ollie told him. Bo felt Mat's body getting heavier, and he'd sunk a little more into him. Dared he hope?

When Ollie placed her small, warm hand on his bare forearm, he looked down into her lovely, sympathetic face. 'I didn't know what to do. What if you weren't here?'

'You would've figured it out. You would've done an Internet check, called a doctor or taken him to an all-night clinic. You would've made a plan,' Ollie reassured him. 'You've got this, Bo. I have faith in you.'

I have faith in you…

Five little words but ones he hadn't heard since

his grandfather, the only person who'd believed in him, had passed. They filled Bo with strength and peace. And, as he watched Ollie walk away, he was terrified of how much he'd liked hearing those words on her lips—how much her good opinion of him had come to mean to him in such a short time.

What he felt for her was sexual, not emotional: he didn't do emotions. Yes, he wanted her—under him, over him, up against the wall. But that was just lust—and nothing else but lust. He needed to remind her of that.

Bo followed her into the hallway and his fingers locked around her wrist. She spun around to face him and he saw everything he was feeling in her rich brown eyes. Desire, need, want and confusion Ollie looked up into his face, raw with need, and she waited for him to speak. He was an articulate guy; why was he struggling to find words? And, when they did arrive, they weren't what he'd intended to say.

'I know that nothing can happen between us, and I would never presume that something could. But... but if I do not taste you soon, kiss you senseless just once, I might lose my mind.'

Ollie knew Bo was waiting for her to say something, to permit him to kiss her. She also knew that if she said no then he would step away and they'd never mention this encounter again. The thing was...she couldn't say no. It wasn't a word her tongue could wrap itself around. Yes... She could manage yes.

She was normally so clear-thinking. How could he confuse her like this? She could figure that out later. Right now there was only one thing she wanted from him and that was for him to push his body into hers and kiss her as fiercely as he could. Ollie lifted her hand and placed it on the back of Bo's neck, surprised at how hot he was. Standing on her tiptoes, she placed her other hand on his chest and placed her lips on his. For a few seconds, she wondered if she'd made a huge mistake, because he stood statue-still.

Then his lips softened under hers, they nibbled and explored, and his hands came up to hold her face, his thumbs gently brushing her cheekbones. But, if this was the only kiss she was going to get from him, she wanted more than her face to be touched, her lips to be explored. She wanted to be so close to him that a sheet of paper couldn't slide between them. She wanted his tongue in her mouth, his hand on her breast and her stomach pushing into his erection.

As if he heard her unspoken demands, Bo changed tempo and Ollie knew the exact moment that the fuse inside him detonated. His hands dropped, one to her breast the other to cup her left butt cheek, and he pulled her up and into him, pushing his shaft into her stomach. His tongue slid into her mouth, hot and demanding, and lust and heat skittered through her. Her nipple bloomed under the swiping motion of his thumb and she groaned when he pushed aside the fabric of her sleeping vest. Sliding her hands under his shirt, she explored his back, running her fingers down the deep valley of her spine, allowing them to drift over his hard, well-shaped and truly spectacular butt. Under her hands, he felt perfect.

'You are so very gorgeous,' Bo muttered, yanking his mouth off hers to mutter the words.

Frustrated because he'd stopped kissing her, she gripped his shirt in her hands and twisted the fabric, lifting her chin and mouth in a silent plea for him to kiss her again. The world stopped and faded away when he kissed her and she rather liked it.

'Bo, kiss me again...' She murmured the words against his lips.

He rested his forehead on hers, his knees bending to make allowance for their difference in height. 'I can't,' he told her, his breath ragged. 'If I start kissing you again, I swear I'll take you up against this wall.'

She simply looked at him, unable to find a flaw in that plan.

'Olivia!' he said, his hands tightening on her biceps. 'This is crazy. We can't—you *know* we can't.'

Why not? There was no one in the house but Mat and he wouldn't care.

Wow, she really was losing her mind. One kiss and she was ready to fall into bed with him, forgetting that he was paying her salary and that she was there to look after his child. Ollie released his shirt and she placed her hands on the wall behind her, her palms flat against the surface. Bo pulled away from her and he gripped her hips with white-tipped fingers. He didn't look embarrassed about his tented bottoms so she figured she shouldn't be either. She closed her eyes and pulled in a few deep breaths until her blood came off the boil and her brain started working again.

Ollie looked away and pulled her bottom lip between her teeth. She'd been unprofessional in the extreme, and if Sabine got wind of this—friend or not, mentor or not—she'd be fired. Thank goodness that this would be her last professional gig: if she messed up and slept with an employer, it wouldn't affect her ability to get any more work. She had work, just not the kind she wanted.

Anyway, you are not going to sleep with your client, Olivia.

Well, she was going to try not to. As hard as she could.

The thing was, nobody had ever made her feel so jittery before, so alive, as if she'd been plugged into a source of universal energy. She just needed to look into Bo's craggy face and the space between her legs heated and her body wanted.

It craved.

Stupid thing. What on earth was wrong with her?

'We can't do this, Ollie,' Bo told her, his voice sounding gruff. 'It was a mistake.'

A mistake. Of all the words he could've chosen to use, that was the one that hurt her the most. It was the word that her parents had used when she'd told them she wanted to go travelling; what Fred had used when he'd called off their engagement; the word Sabine had used when she'd told Ollie she was getting in too deep with Rebecca, as if loving that little girl and giving her all that attention could be a mistake.

Mistake, mistake, mistake.

She'd made so many of them, including trusting Fred and making that deal with her parents to return to work after five years.

No, she couldn't think about the past now. She wouldn't add tears to this already embarrassing interlude. Ollie looked down so that he couldn't see her eyes, silently cursing. She blinked rapidly and, when she was sure they were clear, she looked up again. In the morning, she'd resume her search for a permanent nanny for him, someone to take her place. She needed something to take her mind off what had just happened, and it would also be a good reminder that her position here was temporary and that she was just passing through his life.

Straightening her shoulders, she forced herself to smile. 'That should never have happened, but it did. But maybe we could forget it?'

There wasn't a snowball's chance in a volcano, but it sounded like something she should say.

Bo sent her a '*who are you kidding?*' look. 'We can try.'

CHAPTER SIX

A FEW DAYS LATER, Bo looked out of his study window and watched Ollie move her supple body from one yoga pose to another. Mat sat on the blanket next to her, and Ollie occasionally stopped to hand him a toy or to talk to him. She was incredibly patient and didn't seem to mind that he was interrupting her yoga routine.

Bo was grateful she wore a T-shirt over her brief exercise shorts, ones that hit her mid-thigh, although the shirt didn't cover much when she had her butt in the air. Bo told himself to walk away; he shouldn't be ogling his nanny and thinking about how her amazing body would feel under his hands. If he didn't, he'd walk out there and kiss her senseless again. And this time, he wasn't sure he could stop himself from going past the point of no return. Ollie, inexplicably, seemed to want him as much as he wanted her, so she wouldn't be the one to put the brakes on…

He had the hots for his nanny. It was so tacky, so Hollywood.

Forcing himself to turn away, Bo walked over to

the drafting board in the corner of his study, knowing he needed to get some work done. He'd managed a little, not very much at all, and he was so far behind it was ridiculous. But it was still only the second week since Mat's arrival and he was taking the time for his son to get used to him. And for him to get used to Mat.

On his desk, his phone vibrated and Bo scooped it up, grimacing when he saw his mother's name on the screen. At some point, he'd have to tell her that she was a grandmother and it was news that wouldn't excite her. It was hard enough for her to see and spend time with Bo, and she wouldn't be prepared to give Mat any attention. There was no play in her emotional rope.

He greeted Bridget—he'd started calling her Bridget in his late teens to goad her, but had been quickly informed that she preferred it to 'Mum'. He rubbed the back of his neck as his mother launched into a description of the latest deal she'd concluded and how much money she made. Honestly, he didn't care.

'And you?' Bridget demanded. 'Are you on track to make your third-quarter projections?'

He had no idea. He presumed so. His accountant hadn't told him otherwise.

'Business is good, Bridget.' He grimaced at the design on his easel. It would be a lot better if he could finish his designs.

'You sound distracted, Boland,' she retorted. 'That's not like you. What's happened?'

Bo was not about to tell her about Mat over the phone. No, he'd need to ply her with a couple of martinis first before telling her she was a grandmother.

'I'm fine, just busy.'

She didn't speak for a few beats, and Bo knew it was her way to get him to fill the silence. Nope, that wasn't going to happen. He hadn't fallen for that trick since he'd been eight. Bridget eventually huffed and he easily imagined her blue eyes narrowed with frustration. Bridget didn't love him—he didn't think she even liked him—but she enjoyed the cachet of being his mother. And, like all self-centred people, she hated being out of the loop.

Tough. He hated the fact that she'd never tried to connect with him emotionally.

'So I presume I will see you at the ball tonight?' Bridget said, her voice taking on an extra edge of crispness.

Ball? What ball? 'Sorry, what are you talking about?'

'Darling...' Bo didn't react to the endearment; she called everyone darling. 'It's the social event of the season, and the last before everyone scatters to take their summer holiday. You RSVP'd months ago. I know you did, because I saw Freja's guest list, and you said you would attend with a guest.'

Bridget and Freja, along with a couple of their cronies, were the doyennes of the country's A-list social scene and were not to be crossed. Not if he wanted to keep getting invitations to the events his clients—the rich and famous, the people who were in the market to buy yachts—attended. The balls and cocktail parties were endlessly tedious but his attendance was expected and it was where many a deal was initiated.

'Henry Foo will be there,' Bridget stated, more than a little smugly.

Henry Foo? Really? He was a Hong Kong banker who'd recently purchased the famous Spirit of the East racing team. Bo had heard that Henry Foo was looking to upgrade. The Sørensons had a long history with the Spirit of the East team: his grandfather had designed one of their first winning yachts, and his father another. It would make history if he could design a third, incorporating the newest technology.

'Who are you bringing to the ball, darling? Do I know her?'

Bo closed his eyes and tipped his head back, his hand tightening around his phone. He'd meant to find a date, but he'd forgotten. And he could not rock up at the ball solo: that would a social faux pas, especially at such late notice.

Bo ended the call, swore and rubbed his hand over his face. He was in a world of hurt here, and he mentally ran through his long list of potential dates. It was time to start phoning around…

'Problem?' Ollie asked, walking into the room with Mat on her hip. Before he could answer, his housekeeper called Ollie's name and she turned round. Greta bustled into his study—it was like Copenhagen Central Station at rush hour this morning—and cooed at Mat before taking him from

Ollie. His housekeeper was enamoured by his son and Mat spent a great deal of time with her on the mornings she cleaned his house—somehow she managed to get everything done with Mat on her hip.

Bo looked at the folder in Ollie's hands and knew she wanted him to look at the CVs for a nanny to replace her. The idea made his head, and heart, hurt.

'Well?' Ollie demanded after Greta had left the room. 'What's wrong?'

Bo looked down at his phone and sighed, frustrated. 'I need a date for a function tonight—one I forgot about, and that's very unlike me.'

Ollie rested the water bottle against her flushed cheek and he thought that she looked stunning with her skin flushed pink from exercise. 'It's no wonder you forgot. Mat's arrival was bound to push other less important things out of your head.'

He pushed an agitated hand through his hair. 'Normally I'd send my apologies and blow it off, but I've just heard the hostess has arranged for me to meet a man I want to impress.'

Ollie sat on the arm of the nearest chair and crossed one slim leg over the other. 'You don't strike me as being someone who needs validation. Why this guy? And why do you need to impress him?'

She was so direct, so honest in her questions and pointed in her remarks. He liked her ability to cut through the nonsense and hone in on what was important.

'He's just bought a sailing operation that my family has a long association with. He wants to upgrade with some new yachts and I want to design them. Whenever they've needed a new direction and technology in the past, a Sørenson has provided it. First, my grandfather, then my father. I want to carry on the tradition.'

'Ah, the weight of family expectation,' Ollie murmured. He heard the irritation in her voice and wanted to know how her family annoyed her, wanted to find out more. But, before he could, Ollie spoke again. 'It sounds like an awesome opportunity. You should go.'

That was the plan. 'I need a date.'

Ollie raised her eyebrows. 'Surely you're big enough and old enough and sophisticated enough to attend a function on your own, Sørenson?'

He narrowed his eyes at her jibe. 'I said I'd take a date and that's what I have to do.'

Ollie shrugged, looking unconcerned 'Then you'd better find one.' She shoved her tongue into her cheek. 'If you tell me where to find it, I'll fetch your little black book for you. That's what you older folk use, isn't it?'

Older folk?

'I'm thirty-eight years old,' Bo retorted.

'You are nearly ten years older than me—that's practically a generation.'

He caught the amusement in her eyes and knew she was trying to wind him up. He felt laughter bubbling up inside him and shook his head. He'd laughed more, and felt more, since she'd arrived in his life than he had in the past ten years. Somehow she made his house seem lighter, his responsibilities to Mat not quite so petrifying and she made him think he could be a good dad to Mat.

And she was also the solution to his current predicament. Why should he go out of his way to find a date when a gorgeous woman was standing in front of him? 'Because you made that crack about me being old, you can be my date tonight.'

Ollie held up her hand, her curls shimmying as she shook her head. 'At a ball? Uh…no.'

'Uh…yes.'

Yep, he could easily imagine walking into Freja's incredible Carrera marble hallway with Ollie on his arm, standing at the double-volume doors, waiting for her butler to announce their entrance into the room. She was nothing like the women who normally accompanied him to social events, those cool, haughty blondes who expected the world to stop when they walked into a room. And, if Ollie agreed to go with him, then he wouldn't have to spend the next hour looking for a date, apologising for the late request and stroking some egos. He was an extremely eligible bachelor, and he'd quickly find someone who'd say yes, but he might have to do a small amount of grovelling first.

He really couldn't be bothered. Not when the woman he most wanted to take to the ball was standing right in front of him. Yes, he knew it wasn't a good idea—he was blurring the lines between work and play—but he was tired of downplaying his attraction to Ollie. His hands itched to touch her stunning body and desperately wanted her wide, full mouth under his again. He wanted to hear the hitch in her breath as he pulled her into his body… He didn't know how he'd found the willpower to stop kissing her the other day. The lower portions of his body were still unimpressed.

But getting involved with Ollie—Mat's nanny—would be flirting with danger. Or…would it? Maybe she was the perfect person to have a fling with because her time in Copenhagen was limited. She'd told him that she needed to be back in London at the end of the summer. By then, he'd not only feel far more confident in his abilities to take care of Mat, but the initial excitement of a new relationship—fling, affair—would be starting to fade. They wouldn't have to call it quits because there would always be an end date, a time to stop.

Why hadn't he thought about this before? 'So? What do you say?' he asked Ollie.

Ollie folded her arms across her chest and frowned at him. 'I'm here to look after Mat, Sørenson, not be your last-minute date. And, even if I wanted to go, who would look after Mat while we were out?'

That was easy. He looked past her to see Greta, who was vacuuming the passage with Mat on her hip. His boy looked as if he was having the time of his life. 'Hey, Greta?' he called.

Greta turned and poked her head round the frame of his study door. 'Is there any chance you could babysit Mat tonight if I can persuade Ollie to come with me to the Møller ball?'

Greta's eyes widened in surprise, as he'd known they would. The ball raised millions of euros for good causes and the next day the residents of Copenhagen, and the rest of the country, discussed who wore what, and who went with whom. Greta nodded enthusiastically. 'Of course I will. Ollie, you must go!'

'I don't think so,' Ollie told her.

'But they have fireworks and entertainment, and the food is cooked by one of the country's greatest chefs! You will see one of the oldest and grandest houses in the country.'

Ollie, damn her, still didn't look impressed. 'Even if I wanted to go, which I'm not sure I do, I don't have a dress or shoes or anything like that.'

There were some perks to being a billionaire and one of them was having a personal stylist on a retainer. Carla purchased his clothes, put his outfits together and made sure he never made a fashion mistake. Clothes weren't something he spent a lot of time thinking about. 'If that wasn't a problem, would you say yes?'

Ollie looked like a deer caught in the headlights, a little excited and even more terrified. 'Oh, come on, Bo! There has to be someone else you could ask.'

There were several someones but he didn't want to take any of them; he wanted Ollie to accompany him to the Møller Ball. He wanted to see the house through her eyes, watch her as she marvelled over the firework display, the fire eaters and the trapeze artists. He was a little blasé and a lot cynical—he'd seen and done it all—but maybe, through her, he'd see things a little differently. He held her eyes and waited for her answer. As he expected, she tried another way to wriggle her way out of it.

'I can't ask you to pay for a dress and shoes I will never wear again.'

She hadn't asked him to pay, but he would. He couldn't expect her to fund an outfit suitable for the very lavish function. And, if he never worked again, he had enough money to last several lifetimes. He wouldn't notice the cost of her designer dress or shoes. 'That's not an issue. If you give me your sizes, I will arrange for my stylist to bring over several outfits for your consideration.'

'You have a stylist?' Ollie asked before sighing. 'Of course you do.'

She bit her bottom lip and Bo had to stop himself from crossing the room to her and soothing the bite mark with his tongue. She was as sexy as sin in her skimpy exercise clothes, and he knew she'd look stunning in a ball gown and high heels. Resisting her was a losing battle. It was a good thing that he'd decided to surrender.

'Of course she's going to go,' Greta told him. He'd forgotten that she'd been listening in, that she was still holding Mat. What was it about Ollie? She made the world around him fade away until she was all that remained. Bo rubbed his lower jaw with his hand. He'd thought that Mat dropping into his life had been a life-changing event, and it was, but Ollie's arrival was also causing waves in his previously still-as-a-pond life. He felt as if he were standing in an unsteady bucket in the middle of the Bering Sea.

It was terrifying, exciting and, weirdly, thrilling.

Greta looked at Ollie, pursing her lips. 'She's an eight, foot size UK seven.'

Bo looked at Ollie, waiting for her confirmation. 'She's not wrong,' she reluctantly admitted. Throwing her hands up into the air, she nodded. 'If you can arrange a suitable dress and shoes, Cinderella will accompany you to the ball.'

Eight and seven, clothes and shoes. Do not mix them up or you'll never hear the end of it. 'I think it would be pushing it to call me Prince Charming,' he told Ollie.

She handed him an impertinent smile. 'I didn't,' she pointed out. 'You're more of a *nisse*—or do you call him a *tomte*?'

A *nisse* or *tomte* was a short-tempered troll common in Danish folklore. Bo didn't know whether to be amused at her quick wit, impressed that she'd been reading up on Denmark or offended by the reference.

Unable to decide, he shook his head and picked up his phone to call the stylist and make her very happy indeed.

The stylist brought ten dresses for Ollie to try and in the end she settled for a fluid, sleeveless, blindingly white evening gown with a low neckline and a far too high ruffled slit that exposed her right thigh. A bright-red silk rose rested on her hip and it gave the gown a hint of fun and colour.

Ollie looked at her reflection in the freestanding mirror. The make-up-artist-slash-hairdresser who'd accompanied the stylist had pulled her hair back into a complicated twist and she found it hard to recognise her reflection. She looked sophisticated and stunning, nothing like the down-to-earth nanny she prided herself on being. Her skin glowed and her make-up was light but her lips were the exact colour of the rose on her hip. She looked like someone who would be at home attending a ball hosted by an influential family at one of Denmark's oldest houses, on the arm of the country's most eligible bachelor.

She didn't feel as if she belonged anywhere—not at the ball, not as a nanny and definitely not in London as an accountant. She felt like a fish out of water and had no idea where to find her pond. And what was she thinking, accepting the invitation to accompany Bo to this ball? It was highly unprofessional and she was breaking the cardinal rule of being a good nanny: do not blur the line between the professional and the personal. The problem was that she wanted to get very personal with Bo, as soon as possible.

Ollie glared at her reflection, upset with herself. Yes, Bo was a very good-looking guy—male magazine-cover sexy—and he was smart and successful. But he was her boss…

Normally she wasn't a slave to her libido, and she wasn't someone who galloped into relationships. She took her time and made clever decisions. It took her a while to open up and allow someone behind her walls. It had taken her three months to agree to date Fred, and another two months before she'd slept with him. Agreeing to marry him had required a lot of thought. After a few weeks and many sleepless nights, Ollie had eventually decided they could make their marriage work.

After loving and losing Becca, and realising that Fred was not only an unsympathetic jerk but also a cheat, she'd built her barriers higher and retreated further into herself. She rarely dated and she hadn't had a lover since Fred.

But Bo made her feel things she shouldn't. He made her want, he made her burn and, yes, he made her yearn. He made her feel unsettled and off-balance and she knew she should put more space between them. Because she was fantasising about her boss, because thoughts of him naked bombarded her—him sliding into her and making her sigh and scream— she knew she should be even more professional than she normally was.

So what was she doing, accompanying Bo to this function, allowing him to pay for her dress, her make-up, her hair and the silver three-inch heels on her feet? Why couldn't she stop thinking about how good they'd be in bed? Why couldn't she stop wishing for a repeat, and more, of their fire-hot kiss? She wasn't a woman who lost her head, but he could make hers spin.

If she was clever, she'd pull off this dress, wash her face and tell him that he was going alone, that she was pretty sure the world wouldn't stop turning if he didn't arrive with a woman on his arm. But tonight she didn't want to be Ollie the nanny, she wanted to be Ollie his date, the woman he looked at with masculine appreciation. For the first time in years, she wanted to be an object of desire.

Yes, it was a very bad idea, but she was going to the ball. She hoped she wouldn't end up regretting it.

CHAPTER SEVEN

IN THE SOPHISTICATED, double-height hallway of the Møllers' wonderful house, Bo placed his hand low on Ollie's bare back and thanked the waiter for their champagne. Ollie took hers and lifted the glass to her lovely red lips, and he noticed the fine tremble in her hand.

Around them, elegantly dressed couples mingled in the enormous hallway, caught up in conversation before entering the massive reception room on the right of the hallway. He smiled at an acquaintance and looked down at Ollie's lovely face. Despite her heels, he still had a few inches on her, and he could see the trepidation in her eyes and knew she was feeling out of her depth.

She shouldn't—she looked utterly ravishing. He'd expected his stylist to come up with something nice for her to wear but the ice-white dress against her light-brown skin was stunning and showed off her slim but strong body to perfection. Occasionally the ruffles of her dress would part, drawing attention to a long and shapely leg. She looked ravishing and, yes, ravishing her was something he couldn't wait to do.

Man, he was in a world of trouble here.

Ollie looked at her champagne glass and a smile curved her lips. 'This is great champagne,' she told him. He grinned. It should be: it was a one of the best champagnes in the world. 'You do look lovely, Olivia.'

Ollie tipped her head to the side and lifted her thin, arched eyebrows. 'Olivia?'

He shrugged. Her full name was strong and lovely, gracious even. 'Ollie' didn't suit her, not to-night. 'How did you come to be called Ollie?' he asked, steering her towards the reception area.

'I have four brothers, so I got lumped with a boy's name,' she explained. 'My ex-fiancé called me Olivia sometimes.'

She'd been engaged? Bo tugged her to the side of the room and they stood in front of eight-feet-high windows decorated with pure silk, fuchsia-coloured curtains. Pieces of incredible art dotted the walls but he only had eyes for Ollie. Nothing painted by Reuben or Vermeer could compete with the lovely woman standing next to him. 'How long have you been unengaged?' he asked, trying to sound casual and missing by a mile.

'Ah, for a few years now,' Ollie replied, her eyes not meeting his.

He caught the flash of hurt in her eyes, the twist of her lips. 'What happened?' he asked, confused by his curiosity. He'd never cared about his lovers' pasts before; it had never been a factor, mostly because they'd never lasted long enough for it to be an issue. He was also in his late thirties and knew what had happened before his arrival was none of his business. But, with Ollie, he couldn't help feeling annoyed and a little jealous.

Ollie took her time replying. 'When I needed his support the most, when I needed him to step up and be there for me, to listen and not try to fix the situation, he couldn't give me the support and empathy I needed.'

The sadness in her voice couldn't be missed and Bo knew it had been caused by something other than their break-up. She'd been hurt deeply and her ex's behaviour had compounded that hurt.

'How long were you together?' Bo asked, wondering why he was still asking questions, the conversational equivalent of jabbing a sore tooth with his tongue.

'We met in our first year of university. He dropped out, joined the army and is now a captain in the Grenadiers. We had a very long-distance relationship for most of our time together and maybe that's why it lasted longer than it should've. In hindsight, I don't think we knew each other very well,' she admitted.

'There's nothing like living together to get to the heart of a person very quickly,' Bo said. 'Take us, for instance—you've only been in my life and house a short time, but I know that you need three cups of coffee to wake up, that you are more patient with children than you are with adults and that you are struggling to make a decision.'

Her eyes widened and her mouth dropped open in surprise. 'Why would you think that?' she asked.

She had the worst poker face in the world. 'Eh, it might be the fact that you spend a lot of time staring off into space and you bite the inside of your cheek when you do it.'

A hit of pink flooded her face and she looked younger than her twenty-eight years. 'Well, I've learned some things about you too,' Ollie told him, lifting her chin. Oh, he enjoyed her fighting spirit, and liked that she gave as good as she got.

He leaned a shoulder into the wall, his tuxedo brushing the gilt frame of a Monet. 'Really? Like what?'

'That you are completely in love with Matheo and your emotions scare you. You never expected to love him this much. You thought he would slide into your life and you'd be able to keep your emotional distance.'

Well, yes. It was his turn to feel shocked, but he hoped he hid it better than Ollie did. He considered denying her words but didn't see the point. 'You're right, I didn't expect to feel so emotionally connected to him so quickly.'

'He is your son, Bo, that's what happens between parents and children,' she pointed out.

Not always, he wanted to tell her. Sometimes parents had children and didn't feel much for them. His mother didn't love him. Then again, as the spoiled only child of a media mogul, she'd never been taught to love anybody. His father had never spent any time with him; partying and being seen had been far more important than spending time with his son.

And, at that moment, Bo made a conscious decision, a silent promise that he would never neglect his son the way his father had him. He'd never put himself, or his work, first. But wasn't that what he was doing tonight—leaving Mat with Greta to land a client? Had he already failed his first test?

'Good grief, you look like you've sucked on an ultra-bitter lemon,' Ollie commented. 'Whatever is the matter?'

'I left my son to attend a ball so that I could land a client,' Bo told her, his voice sounding a little strangled.

She nodded. 'Yes, you did. And why is that suddenly a huge problem?'

'I don't want to neglect him, Olivia. I *won't* neglect him. He has to know that he's not second best, or an afterthought, or way down on my list of priorities.'

Ollie placed a hand on his arm, and through his tuxedo and his cotton dress shirt he felt the heat of her hand. 'Bo, when we left Mat was asleep; he doesn't even know that you aren't there. And, while I firmly believe that you as his primary caregiver should spend most of your nights at home, you are still allowed a life. Kids are smart—they know when they are wanted or not—and you spending a night out of the house now and then isn't a big deal. In fact, it's important that you do.'

He kept his eyes on hers, his panic receding at her soothing voice. 'Why?'

'Because, if you don't, you will go off your head. You're a new dad—you were Bo before and, like any single parent, it's not healthy to have your life completely consumed by your child.'

He took her hand and squeezed her fingers, keeping his fingers linked in hers. 'This would be so much harder if you weren't around, Olivia.'

'Well, don't get too used to me—I'll be leaving soonish,' she told him. He thought she'd aimed to sound crisp, but he heard a hint of sadness. Or maybe he was projecting his feelings onto her. He couldn't imagine her leaving, and didn't want to. She'd slid into his life and Mat's without so much as causing a ripple and, in some ways, it felt as though she'd always been there, a part of the furniture and the fabric of the house, in the nicest way possible.

It seemed right to look up from working at his desk in the mornings to see her stumbling to the kitchen, sometimes with Mat on her hip, sometimes without, yawning as she made herself a cup of coffee and working his complicated coffee machine with practised ease even though she was still half-asleep. Watching her do yoga in the garden was a pleasure— she was hot. He often found himself laughing at the silly things she said to Mat, at her dry commentary on her yoga skills.

He'd spent a few mornings at work, at meetings

he couldn't miss, but for the first time in his life his entire focus wasn't on his business, it was on his house and what was happening within it. He frequently wondered what Ollie and Mat were up to and resented time spent away from his son.

And his son's nanny.

No woman had ever intrigued him as Ollie did. No one had ever made him want to scrape that superficial layer and see what lay beneath her smooth skin and within those deep-brown eyes. He wanted to know her history, what made her tick, what twists and turns she'd taken to bring her to his son and him. Why he'd lucked out on having one of the Europe's best nannies looking after his son; the owner of the agency she worked for had been deeply serious when she'd made that claim.

That she was great for Mat was no surprise, and his little boy was calmer when she was around, less anxious. There was something about her energy that soothed, and it didn't only work on his little boy. Sometimes, while working on a design, he'd find himself getting frustrated and he'd lift his head and hear Ollie singing to Mat, or tickling him, their laughter mingling. He'd immediately feel calmer, more focused. When she was around, he felt both energised and relaxed, turned on and laid back. It was as if he existed in two states at one time, something that had never happened to him before.

And he liked her, more than any woman he'd met before. She was funny and smart, and he loved the fact that he didn't intimidate her, that she called a spade a spade and wasn't afraid to point out the mistakes he made with Mat. But, instead of making him feel like he was incapable or clumsy, she gently guided him in all Mat-related tasks, pleased when he got things right or remembered something, and patient when he took a little longer to recall what he needed to do.

He was learning so much from her: not only how to look after Mat's physical needs but how to connect with his son on an emotional level. He'd scoffed when she'd suggested that he spend fifteen minutes reading to Mat before he put him in his cot to sleep— he'd protested, saying he was too young and wouldn't understand. But after two nights Bo had realised it wasn't about the words, or Mat's understanding, but about connecting with his son.

Unfortunately, she still had to remind him to cuddle Mat, something that didn't come naturally to him. He did love him, and understood that he should hug his son, but didn't know how to do it or how often. And that was a huge source of embarrassment. He was a grown man, but he had no idea how to express affection. So he copied Ollie, watching how she wrapped her arms around Matheo's little body and held him tight; how she kissed his cheek, ran her hand over his head and down his arm.

Initially, he'd felt weird, but he was getting better. He had to have this nailed before Ollie left. Mat's next nanny might not be as patient or, almost certainly, he might not have the same connection to her as he did to Ollie. If he didn't learn everything he could from Ollie now, he might be in big trouble down the line.

And why was she so attached to that end-of-summer date? Why couldn't she stay longer; why wasn't she flexible? There was so much he wanted to know about Olivia Cooper, far more than he needed to know about the woman who was looking after his son. Much more than he'd wanted to know about any woman before her.

And that terrified him.

The sound of a gong reverberated through the house and the guests started walking towards the dining room. Ollie, looking nervous again, slipped her hand into his, her fingers interlocking with his.

It was second nature to snatch his hand away, to detach his fingers from hers. His actions were partly because he wasn't affectionate, but mostly because he was in the habit of keeping a certain distance between himself and his female companions in public. There had been so many women in the past who'd tried to give the impression that they were more than friends, that he was their significant other, and hand-holding was something they'd all seemed to have in common. It was a way to silently shout, 'Look, I have him, he's mine'. Shutting down the hand-holding, not allowing them to rest their heads on his shoulder as they talked in a group and keeping his physical distance had been his way of showing the world that she was his date for the evening, not a potential love interest.

Bo looked down at Ollie and saw the hurt in her

eyes, her flushed pink cheeks. He'd embarrassed her, and he hadn't meant to, but he couldn't let her or anyone think that she was anyone special, that she would be the one to snare him, to become the first Mrs Bo Sørenson.

That wasn't going to happen. Marriage and love weren't for him—they couldn't be. Not even with this woman who made him feel so much.

In the ladies' bathroom, Ollie cursed her burning eyes and blinked back her very unwelcome tears. Bo had treated her as if she had a contagious disease, and his jerking his hand away from hers had hurt more than it should have. She'd just wanted some reassurance that she was doing okay, to know that he wouldn't abandon her, but he'd made her feel like Typhoid Mary.

Yes, he was her boss, and maybe she'd stepped over the line, but hadn't this entire evening been one huge experiment in over-stepping? From the moment she'd agreed to accompany him to this ball, she'd jumped over the barrier between professionalism and personal, and now she was paying the price for being an idiot.

She was just the nanny doing the boss a favour.

Ollie looked at her reflection in the huge, framed mirror and thought that the bathroom was more suited to a hotel than someone's house. There were two stalls, two basins, a huge mirror and enough lotions and potions stocked by an exclusive cosmetic supplier to keep the hands of dozens of socialites soft and smooth.

Ollie washed her hands, checked that no mascara had landed on her cheeks and pulled her lipstick out of her clutch bag. She didn't need it but reapplying it would give her a minute, maybe two, before she had to pull up her big girl panties and walk back into that room where she felt she didn't belong.

For the first time in ages, she longed to be home, sitting at the battered table in her parents' kitchen, listening to her *gogo*, her mother's mother, when she'd been visiting from South Africa—recounting yet again how she'd met Nelson Mandela when he'd still been a young lawyer in Soweto.

Her eldest brother had studied in London, eventually become a UK citizen and had opened a branch of his family's business there. Before they'd established their business in the UK, her parents had both been staunch anti-apartheid activists, and people assumed her white dad was the privileged one, the one who'd gone to university. Actually, it was the other way round—it was her mum who came from a wealthy family and had studied at the top university in the country. Her dad's parents hadn't been able to afford to send him to university to further his studies. It was her dad who'd worked a ten-hours-a-day blue-collar job and who'd studied after hours for his accounting degree. As a result, both her parents felt a university education was a privilege and that it was never to be wasted.

Ollie understood where they were coming from

but she wished they'd accept that she'd found something she loved better—okay, she'd never loved accountancy, she was just good at it—and that being a nanny was a good, steady job.

She'd been given five years of freedom, and in return she'd agreed that she would return to the UK and work for their accounting business for five years. It was time to pay the piper.

So, instead of getting herself in a state about the fact that her boss wouldn't hold her hand—*how old was she, thirteen?*—she should give up her dream of buying into Sabine's business and start planning her return to join the London branch of her parents' firm and a life filled with figures. And boredom.

As for Bo, well, even if she wasn't leaving and she was interested in a relationship with him—*she wasn't!*—he didn't do relationships and he wasn't into making any sort of commitments to anybody. According to the many articles about him she'd read online, he only ever engaged in brief affairs. So expecting him to hold her hand, expecting anything from him, was simply stupid.

And she was not a stupid girl. She was a girl who was leaving the country in less than two months and, in time, he'd be just another boss she'd worked for.

But as Ollie walked into that huge dining room, one of the last to sit down at the extra-long table, she saw Bo stand up to pull her chair out, his hot eyes on her face, a small, apologetic smile on his lips. Ollie reluctantly admitted he wasn't someone she'd easily forget.

Or forget at all. Worse than that, he was the one man she'd probably have a lot of trouble walking away from.

Maybe she was a stupid girl after all.

CHAPTER EIGHT

AFTER STANDING BACK to let Ollie into his house, Bo waved goodbye to Greta and closed the front door behind them. Conscious of her aching feet, as she wasn't used to wearing heels, Ollie kicked off her shoes and placed her clutch bag on the hallway table.

She bent over to massage one foot, then the other, thinking that it was his fault her feet were on fire. Despite his refusing to hold her hand, she'd spent half the evening in his arms, being expertly whirled around the dance floor. She silently thanked her *gogo*, who'd ferried her to ballet, tap, modern and ballroom dance lessons for most of her childhood and into her teens. She'd felt many eyes on them, and was grateful that the great and good of Danish society wouldn't judge her for having two left feet.

Picking up the hem of her dress from the floor, Ollie swallowed a yawn. She was in that weird state of feeling both energised and exhausted, and in a few hours she'd be waking up to look after Matheo. Nine-month-old little boys didn't care if you'd spent the night in a fancy dress, drinking lovely champagne:

they wanted a fresh nappy, breakfast and attention. And not necessarily in that order.

Ollie walked from the hallway into the living room, Bo beside her. His hand came to rest on her bare lower back, his thumb swiping rhythmically against her skin, sending flickers of heat and sparks dancing across her skin. Right, so he couldn't hold her hand in public, but he could touch her in private.

She knew she should call him out on his actions and move away from him, but she loved that small connection, the heat he managed to generate with so little contact. She pulled in a hit of his aftershave, an understated scent reminding her of Italian lemons and fresh sea air. He looked gorgeous in his tuxedo. He had that clothes-horse body that was required for male models—wide shoulders, long legs, slim hips—and she could easily understand why so many eyes followed him around the room.

He was a stunning-looking specimen of a male in his prime...

And, man, she wanted him.

She shouldn't—it was such a bad idea—but she couldn't imagine padding down the hallway to her bedroom, shutting her door and going to bed alone.

Ollie hesitated, not sure what to do, and opted to walk over to the floor-to-ceiling window that looked onto the sound. Bo headed down the hallway to where Mat slept in his nursery. She heard his door open and then close a few minutes later.

Mat was asleep and they were alone.

'Would you like a drink?' Bo asked, his deep voice sounding rougher than normal.

She shouldn't, but a drink would give her an excuse to prolong this evening, to spend more non-nanny time with him. She nodded and she heard the sound of liquid being sloshed into a glass. When he approached her, coming to stand next to her at the window, she noticed that he'd shed his jacket, pulled off his tie and undone the top buttons of his shirt. Handing her a glass of cognac, he slowly, oh, so slowly, rolled up the cuffs of his shirt to reveal his muscled forearms. The low light of the single lamp turned the hair on his arms a light golden colour and glinted off the face of his expensive watch.

Ollie sipped, grateful for the burn of expensive liquor as it slid down her throat. She knew she should speak, but the words were stuck in her throat. There were words that she could say—*I want you* and *please take me to bed*—but she knew that if they walked down that road they'd make this situation far more complicated than it needed to be.

She was his employee, he was her boss.

It was unprofessional...

This would be her last nanny job...

All the above was true but she knew she would regret not kissing him, not sharing his bed, for the rest of her life... Being with him was a gift she could give herself.

Ollie watched as he picked up his glass and raised it to his lips. Her eyes met his and he watched her, his eyes hooded and glinting with...was that need? Want? Flat-out desire? A mixture of all three?

She pulled her bottom lip between her teeth, unable to break the eye contact. Needing fortification, she lifted her glass again but Bo snatched it out of her hand and banged it down on the closest table, causing the glass to tip over onto its side. Ollie watched the expensive liquid drip over the edge of the expensive table and hit the hardwood floor. They should clean it up, but neither of them made a move.

Her head felt extra-heavy when she lifted her eyes to look at Bo again, and this time she had no doubt what he wanted. It was in his eyes, blazing across his face, expressed in the tenting of his tuxedo trousers.

He wanted her...

They were about to cross a line, a pretty big one. He caught her hesitation and frowned. 'It's a big step, Ollie,' he stated, echoing her thoughts.

'I know,' she replied. 'But it's one I want to take. Do you?'

His 'oh, yeah' came quickly and those two words, and the relieved sigh he released, were all the reassurance she needed. His hands gripped her hips, pulling her into him. Ollie felt her breasts pushing into his hard chest, the hardness of his erection against her stomach. She wasn't a novice when it came to sex. She and Fred—when they'd seen each other— had had what she'd thought was a very healthy sex life. But she'd never felt this shaky and off-balance with her ex. With Bo's green eyes on hers, she felt as if he was striding into her soul, looking around and taking stock.

His sexy mouth, with its thinner top lip, headed for hers and Ollie realised that this was what she'd been waiting for—more of the heat they'd shared a few days ago. But, while she thought they might've left scorch marks on the wall in the hallway when they'd kissed, it was nothing to being on the receiving end of Bo's unleashed passion now.

This was a grown-up kiss, a '*take everything I have*' kiss, a kiss for the ages, a kiss to measure against for the rest of her life. He pushed his fingers into her hair and held her head to his, and his other hand rested low on her back, keeping the lower half of her body tight against his. She felt captured and enveloped, but she didn't care, and she had no wish to escape.

As his tongue slid into her mouth, she tasted cognac and the faint hint of the cigar he'd smoked before they'd left the ball. But her overwhelming sensation was his need to take her, claim her and make her his.

She'd never been a fan of being possessed, of cleaving herself to a man—she was far too independent and modern-thinking for that. But something in Bo's kiss made her think of plundering Vikings and dominant men who scooped up maidens and threw them over their shoulders.

Right now, she got the appeal. He was elementally male, primordially alpha, and she loved it. She loved the way he was making her feel: sexy, desired and oh, so female.

There was power in being desired so fiercely by a man like this, to feel his impatience in his kiss, to know that you were the one he wanted. Ollie felt like a princess, a goddess, someone who had a great deal more power and allure than she usually did.

Unable to help herself, her hands skated up and down his muscled back, and she pushed her body into his, needing to get closer. She explored his neck with her fingers, allowing his soft hair to slide over her fingers, running her hand over his muscled shoulders. Needing more, needing to feel his skin, she pulled his shirt from the band of his trousers and made a muffled noise when she encountered hot male skin. She enjoyed the sizzle, the way his kiss deepened when she pushed her finger between the band of his trousers and under his briefs. She couldn't get very far, and her hands moved to the front of his trousers, seeking the snap that kept them together.

His hands left her hips to hold hers against his stomach and he wrenched his mouth away to look down at her with glittering eyes. 'Are we doing this, Ollie?'

She knew that if she backed away she would regret it for the rest of her life. For one night she wanted to be the object of his attention, the reason his world turned. She needed to feel him shatter beneath her hands, to know she'd made him gasp and groan.

'I want you,' she told him, deciding to be honest. What was the point of lying when he could see her pointed nipples and her skin flushed from need?

'You work for me,' he reminded her, resting his forehead against hers, his hands still holding hers so that she couldn't touch him. And she wanted to, very much. But she hadn't had sex since she and Fred had broken up three years ago and she never had one-night stands. This was totally out of the ordinary for her and she was winging it here. The only thing she knew was that she couldn't walk away from him, not now, not tonight.

'We are adults,' she told him. 'We can separate work from pleasure. This has nothing to do with my job, with Mat, with why I came to Copenhagen,' she continued. Then she remembered how Bo must normally deal with situations like this. 'This is only about sex, about some bed-based fun. I don't do commitment; I won't do commitment. And I'm leaving anyway...'

She sounded so much more confident than she felt. And why wasn't he jumping all over this? Why wasn't he leading her to his bed? Why was he even hesitating? He was the king of no commitment, so what was his problem?

Deciding that there was nothing else she could say to persuade him, she cupped her hand around his strong neck, lifted her thigh, the ruffled split giving her room to move, and draped it over his hip. Dragging her mouth across his, she whispered against it, 'I need you to take me to bed, Bo. Can you do that?'

She knew he wanted her, and she wanted him—

more than she'd ever wanted anybody or anything in her life—so she decided to stack the odds in her favour. Moving her hand down his chest, she skimmed her fingers over his stomach…yep, there was a six-pack under the fabric waiting to be explored. She cupped him, sighing when her hands couldn't cover the length of him, realising how big he was.

When his eyes deepened, flaring with lust, she knew that there would be no more talk, only action.

This might be a mistake, but it was hers to make and one she would never regret. She needed this experience. She needed to know him in the most intimate way a woman could know a man.

Ollie had used words he normally would—no expectations, no commitments, *blah-blah-blah*—but he was tired of doing the right thing, the clever thing, the sensible thing.

Right now, and for the rest of the night, he just wanted to feel.

All reservations about what they were doing, about this journey of discovery they were embarking on, gone, Bo released the air he'd been holding and stopped fighting temptation, currently wearing a long white dress. All night, he'd imagined, hoped and dreamed of watching the garment pool around her feet, exposing her to his hungry, needy gaze. He was going to get to love her and Bo felt like the luckiest man in the world. But he wasn't about to make love to her in front of this window or on a couch. No, he needed his massive bed, the space to stretch out, to move and to love her properly. They might only ever have this one night, a few hours until morning broke and reality intruded, and he was determined to make them count.

Scooping Ollie off her feet—was that a sigh of relief he'd heard?—he walked her down the hallway to the massive suite of rooms under another high, angled roof. He had a small sitting room and a big bathroom attached to either side of his room but to his mind, most importantly, dominating the centre of the room was his California king. The doors leading onto his private balcony and hot tub were open and in the darkness of the Norwegian summer he could see stars hanging low in the sky, close to the purple sea, and he enjoyed the warm, scented air blowing in from the sea. This was his space, his sanctuary, the place he came to relax. He never brought women back to his house, he always went to theirs—it was so much easier to leave! But it felt right that Ollie was the first woman to share his bed, his space.

When her feet hit the floor, he cupped her face and lowered his lips to hers, keeping his touch gentle. He wanted to savour and sip, to take his time exploring her curves and dips, the secret wonderland that was her body—this undiscovered and wonderful land he'd been given access to. He kissed her again, but her lips were a little hesitant, so he pulled away to look down at her. The difference in their height was exacerbated by the fact that she'd kicked off her sexy heels. He bent his knees so that their eyes were level.

'Are you okay?' he asked. 'Do you want to stop?'

If she said she did, he might just howl. But he'd take her back to her room and leave her there. No was no, no matter how far they'd travelled down this road.

She shook her head, then nodded. She looked as confused as he felt. 'Being in your bedroom sort of broke the crazy spell.'

The crazy spell—that was a good way to describe the wave of lust they'd surfed back in the living room. What they were doing was very real and a little scary, similar to the anticipation he felt when standing on the edge of a steep, untested ski slope, or diving off a boat into the blue ocean. But he also felt so, so alive...

Then Ollie looked up at him with her gorgeous, deep-brown, almost black eyes. 'Maybe we can... you know...just kiss again?'

Yes, they could do that—absolutely. Bo led her to the bed. 'Let's get comfortable while we do that, okay?'

Ollie, unembarrassed, hiked her dress up her thighs and climbed onto the bed, watching as he toed off his shoes and bent down to remove his socks. When he lay down next to her, she rolled into him, half-draping herself across his chest. He dragged his thumb over her cheekbone and explored the pretty shell of her ear. 'You are so beautiful,' he told her, his voice sounding as rough as sandpaper.

'You're pretty hot yourself,' Ollie told him, her fingers sliding inside his shirt to find bare skin. He ran his hand down the bumps of her spine and felt her shiver. Yeah, the heat was building. He pulled the grips from her hair, tossed them to the floor and watched, fascinated, as her hair fell to her shoulders and down her back. He picked one curl up and wound it around his finger, thinking it was so soft.

Wanting her to set the pace, his eyes caught hers again and she smiled, a feminine, secret smile that he recognised as being girl code for '*I'm going to blow your mind*'.

He had no problem with that. He really didn't.

Ollie scooted up onto her knees and held back her hair so that she could kiss him without him getting a mouthful of curls, but he pulled her hand away so that her hair hung like a wavy curtain on either side of their faces. Her curls tickled his cheek and his neck as he plundered her mouth, wanting to get them back to feeling wild and inhibited again. While still trying to kiss him, Ollie fumbled with the buttons of his shirt and, impatient to have her hands on him, he gripped the fabric at his collar and ripped the shirt apart, exposing his chest to her roving hands.

Ollie murmured her approval and her mouth moved across his jaw, down his neck and across his collarbone, tracing the lines of the geometric tattoo that flowed from his right pec across his shoulder.

'So sexy,' she murmured.

'Not as sexy as you,' he countered, meaning every word. And if she didn't get out of that dress, if he didn't get his tongue on her nipples or his hands between her legs some time soon, her dress was going the same way as his shirt. 'How attached are you to this dress?' he asked. He'd paid for it, but that meant nothing; she'd worn it, so it was hers.

Ollie's head snapped up. 'I rather like it. Why?'

He narrowed his eyes at her. 'Then get it off before I tear it off you.'

Yes, he sounded bossy, like the CEO barking orders his staff knew him to be. Ollie just grinned. 'You're bossy,' she told him, amused.

No, he was desperate. 'When I need to be,' he agreed. 'But that dress needs to come off.'

Ollie surprised him by flashing a heart-stopping grin, and Bo put his hand on his chest just to make sure that the organ responsible for pumping blood around his body was still working.

Ollie reached for the zipper under her left arm and, as she pulled it down, the fabric of her dress loosened and he forgot how to breathe. Ollie was almost naked and nothing else was important. Her dress fell to her waist and revealed her perky breasts, and her dark-cherry-coloured nipples. Her waist was tiny and Bo needed to see all of her immediately. Using his core muscles, he placed his hands on her bare hips and lifted her up, out of her dress and onto him, her legs straddling him leaving a frothy puddle of white fabric on his deep-brown comforter.

Ollie, naked except for the smallest and most pointless pair of panties he'd ever seen in his life—they covered nothing but a small strip of her mound—started playing with the snap of his trousers again. Pulling her down, Bo dragged his tongue over her nipple before sucking it against the roof of his mouth. Despite the fabric of his trousers and his underwear separating them, he felt the heat between Ollie's legs burning against his shaft.

He needed to be inside her—now, immediately. He couldn't wait any longer.

He ignored the voice of caution telling him he was feeling too much, that he was too emotionally connected and that this felt like more than sex, more than a one-night stand. He pushed his underwear and trousers over his hips and down his legs. He tossed the garments to the floor and, when Ollie repositioned herself on his shaft, he groaned.

Protection... He needed to find a condom.

'Get those panties off while I track down a condom,' he told her, sounding gruff. He didn't keep condoms in the drawer of his bedside table because he always conducted his liaisons elsewhere. There might be a box in his bathroom cabinet, and there was one tucked into his wallet. But leaving Ollie was proving more difficult than he expected.

She leaned down, gently biting down on his bottom lip, and soothed the tiny sting with the tip of her tongue. 'I'm clean and on the pill,' she told him, her eyes begging him not to leave her, to wait any longer.

He shouldn't; he didn't trust anyone to take care of protection but himself, but he couldn't find the will to move out from under her. He was a father because he'd somehow slipped up with Dani but, strangely, even that terrifying thought couldn't make him shift.

Tired of his thoughts, the constant merry-go-round in his head, Bo used his strength to flip Ollie so that she lay under him. He slid his hand between her legs to check that she was ready for him—she so was. Without hesitation he pushed into her, rocked by the exquisite feeling of skin on skin, being condom-free. She felt amazing, hot, wet and like…

She felt like home.

CHAPTER NINE

It was early the next morning when Bo walked into his bedroom holding two cups of coffee. When he sat down next to Ollie, his big shoulder pressing into hers, she lifted his wrist to look at his Rolex watch. It was shortly after six, and they hopefully had at least an hour together before Mat woke up. An hour when she could be Ollie the woman, not Ollie the nanny.

Ollie wrapped her hands around her mug and stared into the rich, dark liquid, thinking that making love to Bo had been far better than she'd expected, far more intense than she'd imagined. He'd pulled emotions to the surface she'd thought she'd buried three years ago, soft emotions, emotions that dealt with connection, intimacy and like. She was scared to the soles of her feet and beyond. He'd pushed her out of her emotional comfort zone and she felt a little disconnected.

Bo dropped a kiss on her head and picked up his mug from the bedside table. He'd pulled on a pair of pyjama bottoms and a white T-shirt and Ollie thought that nobody had the right to look so hot this early in the morning. Dressed in Bo's T-shirt, the open neck of his shirt falling off one shoulder, she felt she didn't measure up.

Silly, because Bo had told her frequently that she was delicious, gorgeous and that she was heaven in his arms.

Get over yourself, Cooper.

Pushing her curls off her forehead, she sipped her coffee and, when he sat down next to her, she hooked her bare leg over Bo's.

'What are your plans for today?' she asked Bo, turning her head to kiss the ball of his shoulder. When she left this room, nobody would suspect her of having an affair with her boss but here, right now, she could be affectionate.

'I have a meeting with the Hong Kong businessman I met last night at the ball,' Bo told her. He sighed. 'It'll be one of those highly technical and long meetings where we work through all the design elements he wants and needs. He'll expect too much and, as diplomatically as possible, I'll have to explain to him what can be achieved and what can't.'

'And at the end of it you'll get a fat contract to design his new racing yachts.' Ollie had no doubt that was exactly what would happen. Bo didn't fail; he always achieved what he set out to do.

'And you? What are you planning?'

'I might take Mat to the beach,' she told him. 'It's going to be a hot day.'

'I wish I could join you,' Bo replied, sounding

regretful. 'I hate the idea of being cooped up in an office on such a gorgeous day.'

'A few weeks back, you planned on spending most of the summer in your office,' Ollie teased.

His slow smile caused her stomach to do barrel rolls. 'Well, now I've found a better way to spend my time, and wasting the sunlight doesn't seem the wisest course of action.'

Ollie looked away, thinking that she would be leaving as summer drew to an end, when the days grew shorter and the nights cooler.

Talking of...

'Did you manage to go through the CVs of the candidates to take over from me as Matheo's nanny?' she asked him, desperate to get back to reality. And the reality was that in five or six weeks—she'd lost count—she'd be in the UK and Bo and Mat would be here. And they'd have a new nanny in their lives. Because she wanted the best for them—how could she not? They were amazing!—she needed to find the best, most qualified, nicest nanny she could. And good nannies didn't grow on trees.

'No,' Bo told her.

'Good nannies are hard to come by, Bo, and they often secure their next appointments months in advance.'

'I got you at the last minute,' Bo pointed out.

Yes, but she wasn't staying in the game. 'As I told you, you are my last nannying job,' she told him.

He pulled away to look at her, his expression quizzical. 'Have we been that much of a trial that you are chucking it all in?' he asked, and Ollie wasn't sure whether he was being serious or not.

'No, of course not. My last assignment in Berlin was supposed to be my last one, but then Sabine asked whether I'd be interested in spending the summer in Copenhagen. The city, and the lure of a little more cash, was too difficult to resist.'

Bo's eyebrows shot up. 'A little more cash? Damn, woman, your fees are extortionate!'

She shrugged, then grinned. 'But I am amazing,' she retorted.

He slung an arm around her shoulders. 'You are,' he admitted. 'You are brilliant with Mat. But why are you giving it up?'

Needing to put some physical as well as emotional distance between them, Ollie threw back the covers and walked over to the window, sitting down in the window seat. She lifted her feet onto the cushion, bent her knees and rested her coffee cup on one of them. She couldn't think when she was so close to Bo. He turned her brain to soup.

'I'm going back because I promised my parents I would join their company five years after I graduated from university. I am supposed to walk into my new office and start my new career at the beginning of September.'

Bo walked over to where she was and sat down opposite her in the U-shaped window. 'I don't understand,' he said, pushing his hand through his wavy hair. It needed a cut, Ollie noticed, but the longer length made him look young, soft. 'What are you supposed to start work as?'

'An accountant.'

'Right, I remember that you have a degree in accountancy,' Bo commented. 'From which university?'

Oh, just a little one called... 'The London School of Economics.'

He released a sound that was part-laughter, part-snort. 'Of course you did.' He leaned back and placed his ankle on his knee, amused. 'So I take it your parents were less than happy when you decided to become a nanny?'

'If by "less than happy" you mean they went ballistic. They told me that they didn't fund my studies at one of the most prestigious universities in the world—at a huge cost to them, as I still wasn't a UK resident at that time—for me to waste it wiping runny noses and ferrying kids around.'

Bo winced.

'After much screaming and yelling, and me digging my heels in, we negotiated a five-year deal. I could be a nanny for that period but I had to work for the company for five years so that they could realise some return on the investment they made in my education.'

'Mmm.' There was a long pause before he spoke again. 'If you didn't have to return home, would you stay on as a nanny?'

She couldn't with him, not now they'd made love. She shook her head. 'No, I'd buy into Sabine's nanny agency. She's offered me a junior partnership and I'd love to do that.'

'But you can't take the opportunity because your parents are holding you to this deal you made?' Bo asked. 'Have you told them about her offer?'

She hadn't because it wouldn't make a difference. They wanted her in London, working for them. That was what had been decided years ago and Coopers didn't change their minds.

And there was a back story that Bo didn't understand. 'My dad didn't get the opportunity to go to university; it simply wasn't possible,' Ollie explained. 'To him, education is an absolute privilege, not something that should be taken for granted. The fact that I am not using the education they paid for is a slap in the face. They love me, but they don't understand how I can love this more. Looking after children does not have the same cachet as being an accountant. It's a blue-collar job and, working in this field when I have a superlative degree offends them.

'And I feel guilty because my degree cost them so much money, and I haven't used it, nor have I followed the path they expected me to. I feel like I need to pay them back.'

Bo stared out onto the harbour, his brow furrowed in thought. 'I can understand that, to an extent, but you are also allowed to change your mind—to do something you love doing.'

It wasn't that easy. She wished it was.

'Can you not talk to your parents again, have another conversation?' Bo asked. 'Can you not find another solution?'

The issues went so much deeper than the cost of her tuition. It was difficult for people who'd been raised outside of South Africa to understand all the discriminations and humiliations of the apartheid system. As a biracial woman born after the country had become a democracy, Ollie didn't fully understand all the nuances either. How could she? She hadn't lived through the trauma of institutionalised racism, of *apartheid,* as her mother and her mother's family had for generations.

Her mum had been part of the first wave of black students who'd joined formerly white-only universities in the eighties when those institutions, reading the signs of change in the country, had opened the doors to start the mammoth task of educational equality—yet to be completed. In her parents' eyes, education was something that could never be taken from you. Ollie suspected that they thought she'd taken her opportunities for granted—opportunities they'd fought so hard for—and that she wasn't appreciative of the sacrifices they and her grandparents had made for the generations that had followed—there'd been frequent stints in jail and near-constant harassment.

Talking to her parents wouldn't take the guilt away. 'I don't know if it would help, Bo.'

He winced. Then he stood up and bent down so that his eyes were level with hers. 'It's not something you can solve now, so come back to bed.' He pulled her to her feet, slid his hand around her waist and dropped it to cup her butt cheek, to pull her into him. He was erect and Ollie sucked in an excited breath.

'I need to have you again but we're running out of time because another, younger Sørenson is going to start demanding your attention soon.'

Ollie glanced at his watch and realised that he wasn't wrong. They had maybe half an hour before Mat woke up. Since Bo could take her far away from reality to a world where only pleasure existed, she was happy to follow him back to bed.

A week later, in his office, Bo scowled at his phone and released a series of hot curses. His mother, damn her, was demanding that they get together. In her words, she wanted to hear about the woman who'd accompanied him to the Møller ball. Bridget had missed the social event of the season because a potential client had demanded a last-minute dinner meeting. His mother wasn't one to let a ball—or a family or her son—get in the way of a potential deal.

Since his mother never concerned herself with his love life, Bo surmised that the gossips in her circle had noticed the amount of time, and the amount of attention, he'd given Ollie at the ball. His mother wasn't particularly interested in his life but she hated not being in the know...

She didn't suspect that he was keeping bigger news from her...

Bo tossed his phone onto the desk. A month had

passed since Mat had arrived in his life and he'd yet to tell his mother about his son.

And he knew why… Because, while he might be head over feet in love with Mat, he knew Bridget wouldn't be, and he didn't want to see the lack of interest in his son that he'd experienced his whole life.

It was only when he'd hit his late teens that his mother had started to show him any sort of attention, and had made space for him in her busy calendar. When he'd asked her why, she'd told him, with her usual forthrightness, that he'd finally arrived at a point of being interesting. Babies were ridiculously annoying, children even more so, and teenagers were tedious. It was only when he'd became an adult that she'd found him worthy of expending her energy to have a conversation with him.

He couldn't explain Ollie without explaining Mat, not that he needed to. And he wasn't ready for her to meet Mat, not yet. He wasn't prepared to share him with anyone but Ollie. He was too new, too precious, and he wanted to keep him to himself for now.

He would postpone having lunch with his mother for as long as he could and he'd use work as an excuse. After all, it had been her favourite excuse to get out of spending time with him for most of his life.

Bo looked at the designs on his drawing board and pulled a face. Between spending his nights with Ollie and Mat—they'd agreed that they would continue to sleep together until she left to return to the UK—he wasn't getting much work done. This summer was turning out to be less than productive but, in his defence, it was the first summer he'd had a baby.

And a lover who'd lasted more than a week.

And, to be honest, his feelings, if he could believe he was even using the word, were causing him more grief and loss of sleep than his many concerns about being a brand-new father. The line between Ollie as nanny and Ollie as his lover had been obliterated and his house was no longer the same quiet and controlled space it had been before. It was now filled with the sounds of his son laughing, his lover singing—off key—and the smell of her subtle scent perfuming the rooms. In his bed he found an innovative and sexy lover; her enthusiasm for him and how he loved her was such a turn-on. Out of bed, he found a stunningly bright and well-read companion, someone whose mind he enjoyed as much as he did her body.

He was, in a nutshell, temporarily domesticated and the idea scared him to his core.

He felt so at ease with her, calm and in control. Oh, they bickered—Ollie tried anything she could to get out of making coffee in the morning and he'd never met anyone who shed hair as she did. But they argued lightly and he found an excellent way to get her to be quiet was to kiss her.

Ollie, bless her, loved to be kissed.

Damn, he was in a world of trouble here. She was leaving in four weeks, stepping out of his and Mat's lives. There were ten CVs on his laptop, ten potential nannies for Mat who needed to be interviewed.

He wasn't interested in any of them. He only wanted Ollie and couldn't see how he and Mat would go on without her.

But they had to; they would. He wasn't a guy who did commitment. What they had was new, bright and shiny, and his feelings for Ollie were probably more intense because they were mixed up in his feelings for Mat. But he wasn't prepared to expose his son to a relationship that mightn't work. He'd watched his parents' relationship as it had moved through its various stages of decay: they'd started with barbs, moved onto arguments and had then ended in outright hatred.

Then they'd stopped talking and acknowledging each other at all. Bo thought that stage had been the worst of all. Arguing and fighting had meant that there was some emotion involved; dismissing and ignoring someone meant they couldn't even summon the energy to do that. He'd watched and hated the process. He'd never put Mat in the position of having to do the same.

A small part of him wished that Ollie had never dropped into his life, but another part of him was grateful she had. He was a mess of conflicting emotions, something he was very unaccustomed to. He needed her to go, but he wanted her to stay. He didn't want to feel any more for her than he already did, but he wanted to know every last thing about her.

He wanted to make love to her for the rest of his life, but he couldn't keep her in his life...

It was official: he was a mess. And he might just be losing his mind.

Bo turned at the quick rap on his door and turned to see Ollie standing there, dressed in a short navy-and-white summer dress. She wore white trainers on her feet, and she'd piled her hair up into a messy knot on the top of her head. She looked fresh, lovely and, at that moment, far too young for him. Mat sat on her hip, the ear of his stuffed giraffe in his mouth.

'Hey,' she said, resting one hand on the empty pram. 'We're going to Torvehallerne for lunch and to look at the food stalls. I thought that you might like to join us.'

He should stay, should try and catch up on all his work, but he knew he wouldn't be able to concentrate. Wherever Ollie and Mat were was where he wanted to be. And it had been ages since he'd visited the beautiful glass hall with its many food vendors selling local produce, artisanal products and delicious food.

After putting Mat in his pram, Ollie walked towards him, placed her hand on his chest, and stood up on her tiptoe to brush her mouth across his. She pulled away, but he lifted his hand to grip the back of her head to keep her lips in place. One small kiss wasn't enough, he needed more. If he could have laid her down on his couch and stripped her naked, he would have done that too. In Ollie's arms, when her mouth was under his, he forgot everything else. He forgot he had a difficult mother, that he was a single father, that she was leaving…

She made that sexy sound in the back of her throat as his tongue tangled with hers, and her hand curled around his neck as she pushed her slim body into his. He ran his hand up the back of her thigh and, when she lifted her leg, he slid his hand under the dress to cup her butt.

She made him feel powerful, more masculine than he ever had before. How could he be expected to give her, *this*, up?

He deepened the kiss, allowing them to roll away on a wave of passion, to forget they had a baby in a pram, that he should be working and that Greta was somewhere in the house. Nothing mattered but the fact that he was kissing this gorgeous woman...

Ollie pulled back and looked up at him with sparkling eyes. Her breathing was faster than it had been before, and a delicate flush painted the skin of her chest, face and throat blush-pink. 'Wow. If I haven't told you before, you truly are an excellent kisser, Sørenson,' she told him, her smile wide.

Kissing had never been a big thing for him until she'd come along. An orgasm had always been the end goal but, if kissing was all he could get from Ollie right now, he'd take it. He was toast, burned beyond belief.

Ollie tipped her head to the side, her brown eyes narrowing a little in concern. 'What's the matter?' she asked him.

Nothing. And, because his life seemed practically perfect at that exact moment, he knew that everything was out of sync and definitely out of control.

Perfect wasn't—couldn't be!—a gorgeous woman, and his chortling son babbling away to his soft giraffe.

He plucked Mat from his pram and carried him to the window, turning his back to her. He didn't need her to see any emotion in his eyes. He was having a hard time dealing with it; he didn't need to burden her with his feelings. He'd sort himself out without anyone else's input.

Mat threw his giraffe against the glass and it dropped to the floor. Bo picked up the giraffe from the floor and handed it back to him. Mat, who thought this was a great game, tossed it again. 'I'm good,' he told Ollie, tossing the words over his shoulder.

She walked over to him and placed her hand on his shoulder and, through the fabric of his cotton shirt, he felt the gentle heat of her palm. 'Why don't I believe you?' she asked softly.

He couldn't tell her that he felt as though he was too big for his skin, as though any room that had her in it was the perfect place to be. It was too much and too soon, and he had to regain a measure of control.

He needed his old life back—he felt in control there.

And, thinking about his old life, he stumbled across a subject that would blow all his warm and fuzzy feelings away. 'My mother wants to meet me for lunch or dinner,' he said, standing up.

'Could you sound more unenthusiastic if you tried?' Ollie asked him.

Fair point.

'Does she want to see Mat?' Ollie asked.

Bo pulled a face and Ollie placed a hand on his arm. When his eyes met hers, he saw the astonishment on her face. 'You haven't told her yet?'

He shrugged.

'Bo, you need to tell her she has a grandson!' Ollie chided him. 'And the longer you leave it, the harder it will be to tell her. What's the problem, anyway?'

Oh, only that if she ignored Mat as she had him his heart would break all over again. 'He's not someone my mother will be excited about,' Bo told her, walking out of his office and towards the front door, Ollie following him out.

'Well, you can't keep him a secret,' Ollie pressed, still looking confused. 'Why don't you invite her to supper tomorrow night?'

No, he wouldn't have wrapped his head around her meeting Mat by then. 'I think the queen of Sørenson Media needs more than a day's notice,' he told Ollie. 'Her calendar is booked up months in advance.'

'She said she wanted to meet you for a meal,' Ollie pointed out, sounding ridiculously reasonable. 'Choose the venue, here or somewhere else, and introduce your son to his grandmother, Bo.'

He heard the order in her voice, the note of *don't mess with me*, and wondered why it didn't annoy him. He was usually too alpha to listen to anyone, and he hated taking orders. That she thought she could order him about was too funny for words; she was tiny and he out-weighed her by a hundred pounds.

What wasn't funny was the fact that he was going to do exactly as she said.

He was in a huge amount of trouble here…

CHAPTER TEN

OLLIE MADE IT a habit to give everyone a fair chance, and she tried not to dislike people without getting to know them, but Bo's mum, Bridget, was the exception to that rule.

She did not like her—at all.

In Mat's nursery, she walked the length of his too-small room, holding the sleeping baby in her arms. It had taken her a long time to get him to settle, and she'd yet to place him in his cot. Mostly because she thought that, if she did, she might use her free hands to wrap them around Bo's mum's throat and squeeze it.

Ollie glared at the mobile hanging over Mat's bed. She'd encountered many rich people in her line of work, her employees and their friends, and she'd dealt with more snobs than most people should. She'd encountered the snooty and the disdainful, the bossy and the belligerent, but Bridget took the cake.

She was truly awful.

Dear Lord, she felt sorry for whomever got her

in the mother-in-law lottery draw. Warm and engaging she was not...

She'd given Bo some space to talk to his mum about Mat, to explain how he'd come to have a son. She'd taken Mat out into the garden but their raised voices had drifted out through the open windows, and Ollie could tell that Bo had been doing his best to keep his temper. Bridget had demanded to know how he could be sure Mat was his kid—even though he was his spitting image!—whether he'd done a DNA test and whether there was anyone else who could take Mat.

He was a little boy, Ollie wanted to howl, not an unwanted box of family keepsakes! How would having a child affect his business? What would Bo be sacrificing by taking on the challenge of raising him? It had taken all of Ollie's willpower not to storm into the house and strip sixteen layers of skin off her boss's—and lover's—mother.

When Bridget had deigned to be introduced to Mat, she hadn't taken him in her arms, neither had she touched his cheek or his hand. She'd admitted that, as far she could remember, he looked a little like Bo when he'd been a baby—but Bo's nanny would know better—and she supposed she would have to add him to her birthday calendar. But Bo shouldn't expect her to babysit, or for her to have much to do with him. As she'd told him on more than one occasion, children only became interesting when they became adults and were no longer a drain on her finances.

She'd heard of tall, cool blondes but Bridget was a solid block of ice.

'You're still frowning,' Bo said, stepping into the nursery.

Ollie looked past his broad shoulder to the open door. 'Is she gone?' she whispered.

'Yep. Her driver collected her,' he replied in a normal tone of voice. 'Fun, isn't she?'

Ollie grimaced. She knew he was trying to make light of his mother's rudeness, and her lack of interest in Mat, but she'd picked up the hurt in his eyes, on his face. 'How did she manage to raise you?' Ollie demanded as Bo took the sleeping Mat from her to cuddle him.

'I mean, you aren't extroverted—you're much too implacable to be that—but you do have a sense of humour and know how to laugh.'

Bo kissed Mat's forehead. 'She didn't raise me. A series of nannies did. And I spent a lot of time with my grandfather, my father's father, the man who started our boat-building business. He was awesome.'

Bo sat down in the rocking chair next to the cot and Ollie perched on an ottoman in front of him. She watched as he leaned his head back and closed his eyes. Ollie thought that the mental snapshot she took of Mat and him could be a perfect advert for something baby-related. A hot guy and his gorgeous son: they'd move a ton of product.

'I guess she's the reason I decided not to have kids,' Bo said, his voice softer than before. 'She and my father are the reason I decided to live my life solo.'

Ollie leaned forward and clasped her hands together. 'They weren't good together?' she asked.

Bo shrugged. 'I don't know if my father made her cold, or her coldness made him stay away, but they were horrible together. They were one of those couples who brought out the worst in each other.'

Ollie wrinkled her nose. 'How?'

'My mum was demanding and ambitious and she thought, probably correctly, that my father should work harder, do more, make more of a splash and be more ambitious. But he liked to work a little and party more. He thought she should relax a little, take some time off and be a wife and mother, and not a robot. He had a point. But neither would compromise, so Bridget worked even longer hours so that she didn't have to come home to an empty house.'

'A house you were in,' Ollie pointed out.

'But I wasn't *interesting*, Ollie, I didn't get to be interesting until I hit my late teens and twenties and became—in her words—less needy. And my father didn't come home because there was fun to be had, and warm and willing women who were prepared to share that fun with him.'

'And you were caught in the middle,' Ollie observed.

Desolation hit his eyes. 'I was never in the middle. I was relegated to the outskirts of their lives. Neither of them could be bothered with me, and each thought I was the other's responsibility. I never wanted to be in the position of wanting love, looking for love and not getting it again. So I made up my mind to devote my attention to my business and my work, and to live my life by myself.'

Sure, Ollie had had her disagreements with her parents about her career, but she'd always felt part of a family, and she felt loved. A few couples she'd worked for had had marital issues but nothing so bad that the kids had been affected. Or at least, she didn't think so.

But she knew that children picked up on emotion, and they could read a room better than any adult. Having met Bridget, she now understood on a fundamental level why Bo had so many reservations about falling in love, marriage and commitment. He'd only ever seen the very worst of what people who said they loved each other could do. Love, to him, meant pulling people down, not building them up.

How horrible.

'I don't want to mess Mat up the same way I was messed up, Ol. I want him to grow up feeling secure in my love—I want him to know that he *is* loved.'

Ollie heard the break in his voice and could see the emotion bubbling through the cracks in his facade. If he lowered some of his shields and broke a hole in his castle-thick wall, people would see the sensitive, loving and thoughtful side behind the alpha man he presented to the world. The man worried about how good a father he'd be, who worried whether he'd do right by his son.

She leaned forward and placed a hand on his

knees, her thumb digging into the hollows of his knees. 'There are no perfect parents, Bo, of this I am sure. But the smart parents, well, they take the lessons they've learned from their parents—or identify the way they were messed up—and try not to inflict the same pain on their kids. That's not to say they won't make mistakes, but hopefully they won't make the *same* mistakes.'

She, for instance, wouldn't put provisos on her kids' education. Her job would be to have her kids educated—their job would be to use or not use what she'd give them.

'I just figure that, whatever my parents did, I'll just do the opposite. I figure I can't go far wrong,' Bo stated, sounding infinitely weary.

That was a good place to start and Ollie told him so. She stood up and bent down to place a kiss on his cheek. 'Just love your son, Bo. Honestly, that's all he needs. I'll see you in bed.'

She walked out of the room to give him some time alone with the bundle of wonderfulness that had dropped into his life.

Later that evening, and after a few hours of losing and finding herself in Bo's arms, Ollie rolled away from him, immediately missing his warmth and the length of his strong body against hers. She'd never had such good sex, had never felt so intimately connected with a man, before. His eyes were closed. Picking up a T-shirt of Bo's, she slid it over her head and walked out of his bedroom.

She needed to rehydrate.

After checking on Mat and dropping a kiss on his head, she padded to the kitchen and pulled a bottle of water from the fridge. Cracking the top, she swallowed half the bottle and stared out into the night. The last few hours—and weeks!—with Bo and Mat had been sublime, a step out of time and completely wonderful.

But it wasn't real life.

Ollie rested the water bottle against her forehead and pulled in a deep breath. She was grateful she'd only met him on her last nanny job and sleeping with him wouldn't affect her professional life. Oh, she doubted Bo would tell anyone they'd slept together, but she knew she'd stepped so far over the line that it was out of sight.

Professionally, that was. Personally, her body was singing. She felt both relaxed and energised, sleepy and excited. But, more than anything, she wanted to stay in his bed for as long as she could and keep loving him.

She felt so comfortable with him, so at ease in her body, happy to tell him what she liked or didn't. There was a freedom with him that she'd never felt with Fred—she'd been so worried about disappointing him. With Bo, she felt as if she couldn't let him down, that everything she did, liked or responded to was fine. Maybe it was because he had a whole bunch of tricks up his sleeve, and Fred had been a bit of a one-trick pony.

Either way, she felt sexually emancipated, as if

she'd been given the freedom to explore. It was liberating and rather lovely.

But she had to be careful that she kept her emotions in check, that she didn't allow like to bleed into love, that she guarded her foolish and impetuous heart. As lovely as this was, whatever it was, Bo wasn't a long-term prospect. Even if she hadn't been returning to the UK in a few weeks, he'd made it very clear that he didn't do commitment and that he wasn't looking for a long-term lover.

She'd been warned and if she fell for him, if she allowed her heart to come to the party, she'd have no one to blame but herself.

Ollie swallowed some more water.

Be wise, Olivia, be strong and do not do anything stupid. Sleeping with him was a choice. If you get hurt, you can only blame yourself. Sex is sex, love is love...do not muddle the two!

'Can I get one of those?'

Ollie jerked her head up and blinked. Bo stood in front of her, dressed in a pair of black cotton sleeping shorts, his chest bare and his hair mussed. Why hadn't she heard him approaching? Really, the man should wear a bell around his neck to warn her of his approach. Nobody should move that quietly; it was against the law of nature...

'Okay, she's spaced out,' Bo said. He stepped towards her, banded his arm around her waist and lifted her off her feet, swivelling her so that he could open the door to the fridge. Still holding her feet off the ground, he used his free hand to pull another bottle of water out of the fridge and kicked the door closed with his foot. Then he put Ollie down in the exact position in which she was standing before.

'You can't just move me around like I'm a piece of furniture,' Ollie complained, but there was no heat in her voice. Honestly, she rather liked it.

And, judging by his small smirk, Bo knew it. 'You're as light as a feather so it's easy to do,' he told her, opening his bottle of water. He drank deeply before sitting on a stool next to the granite-topped island. 'Are you okay? You were miles away.'

Ollie nodded and sat down next to him, placing her bare feet on the rungs of his chair. The inside of Bo's knees touched the outside of hers and she instantly felt anchored and safe. She ran her finger up and down the side of her bottle, collecting condensation on her finger.

They sat in silence for a while and Ollie was surprised by how comfortable it felt. There was no need to rush in with chatter, to make inane comments or to issue platitudes. There was freedom in saying nothing, in being comfortable in silence, and she revelled in it. In most of the homes she'd lived in, ad in her childhood home, people had spoken all the time, and a lack of noise had meant an argument or that there'd been an issue.

With Bo, it just felt peaceful.

Maybe if she and the De Freidmans had sat with their grief a little more, allowed it to have its space and time, instead of filling their days with people and being busy, they might've handled Becca's death better. There was such power in sitting with your emotions, not having to explain them or validate them or, more importantly, push them away. Whether it was a new sexual experience or the loss of a young life, feelings and people shouldn't be contained by boxes, have time frames or be squashed into what society demanded.

Bo ran his hand down her arm and linked his fingers with hers. 'You have very loud thoughts, Olivia.'

She smiled at him, knowing that he wasn't demanding to know where she was mentally but that he'd listen if she needed to talk. 'I was just thinking how wonderful it is to sit in silence.'

Ollie placed her chin in her hand, grateful he hadn't turned on any lights when he'd entered the kitchen. In the semi-darkness, she felt as if she and Bo were in a cocoon, a bubble, a place where they temporarily couldn't be reached by anyone outside of this house by the sea.

'Maybe if I'd taken a little more time to sit with my thoughts and my grief I would've coped better,' Ollie stated. She turned her head to look at him. 'Do you remember me telling you that there's a reason I only stay three months with a family?'

'Yeah,' Bo replied, his voice sounding deep and rich in the semi-darkness. It sounded like dark, rich chocolate tasted...

I would kill for chocolate right now.

Bo left his seat and she frowned when he headed into the pantry. When he returned, holding a bar of chocolate, she realised she'd spoken aloud. Bo ripped off the packaging and handed her the bar so she could snap off a square…or six.

She saw that it was white chocolate and not dark, her preference. She shook her head. 'I don't think we can be friends any more, Sørenson,' she told him, shaking her head. 'White chocolate—really?'

'I gather you are a dark chocolate girl?'

'The higher the cocoa content, the better,' she replied, squinting down at the bar. 'Is there any cocoa in white chocolate? This is mostly sugar.'

He tried to pull the bar out of her hand but she held on tight. 'You don't have to have any if you are going to lift your nose at my chocolate choices,' he told her, trying, and failing to sound sniffy.

'Now, let's not get carried away,' Ollie told him. It wasn't Belgian chocolate, but she'd deal. She snapped off two blocks and popped one in her mouth. It was sweet, too sweet, but that wouldn't stop her from eating the second piece.

Bo grinned at her before breaking off his own piece. 'You were about to tell me why you only take on three-month contracts.'

Ollie wrinkled her nose. Right, they were back to that. But she didn't mind: she wanted Bo to know. And that felt strange because it had taken all her courage to tell Fred that Becca had died: she'd been so worried about his reaction and hadn't wanted to fight when she'd barely been holding it together.

'I was with a family, two older boys and a four-year-old girl, for about six months when the little girl—her name was Becca—was diagnosed with a fast-spreading, virulent brain tumour.'

Bo placed his hand on her knee and squeezed. He didn't need to express his sympathy. It was there on his face.

'There are some families where you are simply the nanny, another staff member, and then there are families where you become another member of that family. I loved them all so much, and they loved me. And I adored Becca. We had this instant, crazy bond.'

Ollie went on to explain that she'd often taken Becca to her chemo treatments due to her parents' demanding, high-powered careers. She had walked the passageways of the hospital when she'd had exploratory surgery, and then again when she'd been admitted with pneumonia because her little body had been so immune-compromised. She explained that she'd played with her, held her, slept in her bed and that Becca had become like a daughter. And she tried to explain how her soul had crumbled when she'd passed away.

'Her parents had each other and, strangely, they coped with her passing better than I did,' Ollie explained. 'I'm not saying they didn't suffer—they were eviscerated—but I felt pretty alone after her death. They took comfort in each other, their sons and their work, but Becca had been my work. And my fun. I felt like I'd been picked up in a tornado and didn't know where to go or how to land.'

'Did your family support you? Your fiancé?'

Ollie shook her head. 'I don't talk to my family

about my work because we always end up fighting about what I do. As for my fiancé, well, he couldn't understand why I'd let myself become so involved, and he thought I should just get over it.'

Bo's expression told her what he thought about Fred's response.

'About a month after Becca's funeral, the De Freidmans asked me to leave. They said that my being there was too difficult and that they needed a clean break. They'd decided to move to the States to start a new life and I wasn't invited to accompany them.' She recalled every minute of that excruciatingly hard conversation, how incredibly sad they'd looked but how determined; how they'd all cried. 'I knew, intellectually, that it was the best thing for all of us, but emotionally I felt like they'd ripped the rug out from under my feet. I was devastated on top of being devastated.'

'Sweetheart,' Bo murmured, the endearment rumbling over her. Ollie was so grateful he didn't spout any clichés. She just needed him to listen and not try to fix the situation, or her, as Fred had.

'They left and I told Sabine that I couldn't do another long-term placement. I knew I couldn't put myself in that situation where I could get so attached again. I knew it wasn't healthy for me. I've been offered many long-term assignments, but I've turned them all down, because I simply couldn't take the risk of falling in love again.'

She saw an emotion she didn't recognise flicker in his eyes and, assuming that he disagreed with her, as Fred had time and time again, she lifted her chin. 'It's not only men and women who fall in love,' she told him, her voice taking on a hint of bitterness.

'I'm not judging you, Olivia,' Bo told her, keeping his voice even. 'Actually, for the first time in my life, I now understand how it's possible to walk around with your heart in someone else's body. That's how I feel about Mat. I didn't know about him, then I did, then he came to live with me and boom! I was head-over-heels crazy about him.'

She nodded. 'I know that I wasn't Becca's mum, but that's how I felt about her.'

'Tell me about her,' Bo said, gripping the sides of her bar stool and pulling her closer to him so that she was enveloped by his long legs, sharing his breath. He ran his fingers down her cheekbone and tucked a long curl behind her ear. His touch was pure comfort, and Ollie sighed. She wanted to tell him about Becca, probably because she'd never spoken to anyone else about her.

So she told Bo about the red-headed little girl with a face full of freckles and eyes the colour of a summer sky. How she'd loved owls, Willy Wonka and the colour purple. How brave she'd been when she'd been prodded and poked, how stoic she'd been about facing death. She'd known and she'd been so accepting, so gracious...

Light and love... Becca had been an old soul in a new, broken body.

When she finally stopped talking, maybe an hour later, Ollie realised that her face was wet with tears. When her words petered out, he reached for a dish towel left in a crumpled heap on the island and gently, oh so gently, wiped her tears away. Then he picked her up, held her against his chest and took her back to his bed, where he loved the hurt away.

By allowing her to speak, to cry, he'd washed away her grief. Oh, it was still there—it always would be—but it was cleaner, lighter, brighter. And it was the best and biggest gift she'd received in a long, long time.

CHAPTER ELEVEN

OLLIE, WITH MAT on her lap, sat at an outside table in the Tivoli Gardens, watching crowds of people as they walked by. She and Mat were enjoying the sights and sounds of the amazing garden. Mat seemed fascinated by the bright colours and the happy faces, and many people smiled at the cheerful little boy dressed in his red-and-white-striped T-shirt and a pair of denim shorts.

Ollie was also fizzing with excitement.

On social media this morning she'd seen that one of her favourite colleagues, an older woman she'd met during her first job in France, was in Copenhagen on holiday with the family she worked for.

Taking a chance, she'd messaged Helen and had been thrilled when she'd told Ollie she had the morning free and would love to meet anywhere Ollie suggested. They'd settled on meeting at one of the many coffee shops in the Tivoli Gardens, and Ollie couldn't wait to see her.

A few minutes later, Helen's short and round figure stepped out from behind a group of teenagers and Ollie jumped up, squealed and placed Mat on her hip. With her free hand, she wrapped her arm around her old friend and breathed in her familiar scent. At nearly twenty years her senior, Helen had married young and, when her husband had died suddenly, she'd become a nanny, and she'd been with only two families since she'd started her new career.

Because she adored babies, Helen immediately took Mat from Ollie and, after sitting down, sat him on the edge of the table, her hands on his stout waist as she cooed at Bo's baby boy.

'He's gorgeous, Ol,' she told her, smiling. Ollie noticed Helen had more grey in her hair but her eyes were the same steady blue, sharply intelligent and full of fun. 'He's going to be a looker when he grows up.'

'You should see his dad,' Ollie told her.

Helen's gaze narrowed and she immediately understood Ollie's subtext. 'You're attracted to him?'

How could she not be? Not wanting to tell Helen that she was sleeping with her boss five minutes into their conversation—though Helen would winkle it out of her at some point, she was sure—she asked Helen about her family and how she was.

After Helen's explanations were over, they placed an order for coffee and *brunsviger*, a cake-like dough covered with a thick drizzle of melted brown sugar and butter. It was one of Denmark's speciality pastries. Taking over as she always did, Helen placed a sleepy Mat in his pram, found his bottle of milk, handed it to him and nodded her approval when the little boy sucked it down while he watched the world out from under the shady roof of the pram. Ollie noticed his heavy eyelids and knew he'd be asleep before he finished his bottle. Mat was a heavy sleeper and could sleep anywhere and through anything. Once he was asleep, she and Helen would have some time to talk.

Their coffees were delivered and they ate most of their pastry; Ollie knew she'd have to go for a run later to work off all those extra calories. Afterwards, Helen leaned back and folded her arms across her ample chest. 'So, what's worrying you, darling?'

So much. Bo, leaving Mat—she was far more attached to him than she wanted to be—going back to the UK, her parents and their insistence that she join the firm.

Ollie sighed, picked up her phone and flipped it over then over again. 'I wasn't supposed to take this job, did you know that?'

'Sabine said something about you giving up the nanny's life and going home to become a career girl.' She wrinkled her nose. 'A lawyer?'

Ollie sighed. 'Accountant.' She picked up her water glass and took a sip. 'My parents are expecting me to join the family firm in September.'

'And I can see you are brimming over with enthusiasm to do that,' Helen replied, sounding sarcastic. 'Just tell your family that you don't want to work for them. Sabine mentioned the possibility of you becoming a junior partner in the agency.' She should be cross about Sabine and Helen discussing her but they were her best friends, her mentors, and they both thought of her as a younger sister. 'She said something about you buying a small share and then working with her for a couple of years until she retires. Then you could buy out the rest of her shares or she could stay a silent partner.'

'That's the dream,' Ollie said and released a heavy sigh.

'I want to hear why you're not jumping at this opportunity, but first a question—wouldn't you need to live in Paris to run the agency?'

Ollie shook her head. 'Not necessarily. I can be based anywhere in Europe. With video calling, we can run the business virtually to a large extent. I mean, I would have to go to Paris occasionally, but I wouldn't have to relocate there.'

'So, what's the problem, Ol?'

Ollie looked at her. 'I know that Sabine offered the same opportunity to you a while back. Why did you turn it down?'

She smiled. 'Because I want to be involved with the kids, I don't want to run a business. You know I don't do this for the money—' Helen had inherited a bundle from her late husband, a stockbroker '—and I like being a part of a family. But also separate.'

Ollie nodded, preparing to explain why joining the agency wasn't possible.

'When I graduated, I promised my parents I would return to the business and work for them. I struck that deal.'

Helen wrinkled her nose. 'And can that deal not be renegotiated?'

Ollie explained her parents' deeply held beliefs that education was a privilege, not a right. And that they had the right to demand a return on the investment they'd made by paying for her education.

'But you are not an investment.'

Ollie touched her hand, not wanting her to think badly of her parents. 'They love me, they do. It's just one thing we disagree on. And it'd be more than saying I don't want to do this: it's about sticking to my word and not trying to move the goalposts because they don't suit me any more.'

'The weight of parental expectation can be a heavy load to carry,' Helen said, her expression serious. 'Have you told them that you don't want to be an accountant?'

'Not in so many words. I guess I don't want to disappoint them more than I already have.'

'I'd talk to them if I were you, Ol.'

That was so much easier said than done.

Helen snagged her uneaten quarter of *brunsviger* and popped a piece into her mouth. 'So delicious,' she murmured. 'So, you are only in Copenhagen for another month or so?'

Ollie was grateful for the change of subject. Thinking about her parents and leaving gave her a headache. 'Roughly, yes. It's a stunning place and I've loved every minute.'

Helen leaned back and crossed one leg over the

other. 'I watched you for a while before joining you. You seem besotted by Mat.'

Ollie's eyes snapped up to her face and Helen just lifted her eyebrows, as if waiting for an answer. When Ollie didn't reply, she spoke again. 'I've been quite worried about you since Becca died, Olivia.'

She didn't want to talk about her parents, and she definitely didn't want to talk about Becca. But, judging by the stubborn look on Helen's face, they were going to have this conversation whether she liked it or not. Since Helen had taken many late-night calls and listened to her sob before and after Bec's death, Ollie couldn't cut her off at the knees. 'You've become attached to Mat,' she stated in her no-nonsense way.

And to his father. Ollie wanted to disagree, but she couldn't. 'I'll still be able to leave,' she told Helen. 'It's not a big deal.'

She was simply looking after Mat, and she was simply fiercely attracted to Bo. It was nothing she couldn't handle.

She hoped.

'Good grief, Olivia, please tell me that you haven't fallen for his father?' Helen demanded, reading the truth in her eyes and on her face.

She couldn't, so she stared down into her cup and closed her eyes. Helen whispered a curse, a word she wouldn't have thought that Helen knew, and she opened one eye to see her friend frowning at her. She lifted her hands and shrugged. 'He's gorgeous and nice and, as soon as I saw him, the room shrunk and the air disappeared and I got shivery.'

Helen placed her hand on her forehead and groaned. 'That bad, huh?'

'That bad,' Ollie confirmed. 'Look, please don't give me the "*it's so unprofessional*" lecture. There's nothing you can say that I haven't told myself. It is stupid, irrational, crazy but, given the circumstances, I'd do it all over again.'

Helen nodded, pulled in some air and caught the waiter's eye. She ordered two glasses of wine and an espresso. Ollie pointed to the sleeping Mat. 'I can't drink wine, I'm on duty.'

'Who said they are for you?' Helen demanded. 'It's my day off and I'm drinking your share.'

Fair enough, Ollie conceded.

'Please tell me that you aren't thinking of making this a long-term arrangement, Olivia?'

She wouldn't dare. Partly because Helen would rip her head off but mostly because she knew that she couldn't stay with Bo, working as his nanny and being his lover. The balance of power was out, and she couldn't live like that on an ongoing basis. 'If I stayed with him, I'd expect a commitment, some promises, all the things that Bo can't give me,' she told Helen.

Helen released a sigh. 'At least you aren't looking at this with stars in your eyes.'

As if! She was smarter than that. 'No, I'm leaving and he knows it. I think that's why he's with me, because there is a finite end to our relationship. But

I do need to find Bo another nanny, someone to replace me. I keep shoving CVs in front of Bo's face
but he won't look at them.'

'Have you explained that finding a good nanny on
short notice is practically impossible?' Helen asked.

'I have, but I think he thinks that, because he
found me at the last minute, he'll be able to do that
again.'

'Not going to happen,' Helen stated. She thanked
the waiter, who placed the wine in front of her, and
lifted her first glass to toast Ollie. 'So what are you
going to do, Olivia? Are you going back to London
and are you going to talk to your parents?'

Nobody seemed to understand that there wasn't a
way out for her, that going back to the UK was what
she *had* to do. 'I made my parents a promise, so it's
back to London to accountancy for five years. Maybe
after that, I'll open up an agency.'

'But by then you'd have been out of the game for
a while.'

Ollie rolled her eyes. 'You are such a ball of optimism, Helen. Thank you.'

'Mmm,' Helen replied. Then she slapped her hand
on the table and nodded decisively. 'I have faith that
you'll work something out, that something will
change.'

'At least one of us does,' Ollie told her, looking
longingly at Helen's glasses of wine.

The island of Bornholm was possibly the most
beautiful place she'd ever seen, Ollie decided as Bo

pulled into a lookout point on the east side of the
island. Below them was a red-roofed town and she
could see a harbour blasted into a rocky outcrop.
The town, like so many others they'd seen, looked
quaint, quirky and utterly lovely.

It was too beautiful a day to spend another minute in Bo's luxurious SUV, so Ollie left the car and
spun round, taking in the green forests and the blue
water in front of her.

'Where are we?' she asked Bo, who was walking
round the bonnet of the car to join her. Mat was fast
asleep in his car seat and Ollie sighed when Bo stood
behind her and wrapped his arms around her waist.

'That is the town of Gundjem,' Bo told her. 'My
holiday house is a ten-minute drive from here but I
wanted you to see this view.'

On the drive, she'd done a quick Internet search
about the island of Bornholm. It was called 'the sunshine island' and Ollie could see why. The light was
incredible, bright and pure. 'The island looks laid
back.'

'It is,' Bo told her. 'I like to think that God was in
a particularly good mood when he created this place.
It's exceptionally pretty with its rocky cliffs, moun-
tains and dense forests. It also has really friendly
locals and great food.'

Ollie couldn't wait to see more of the island and
was so grateful that she'd get to do it with Bo. She
was making memories she'd never forget. 'Do you
come here often?'

'Not as often as I should, but I did spend a lot

of time here when I was a child,' Bo replied. 'The house was my grandfather's and I spent every summer here. I inherited it when he died.'

She was so lucky to get to spend time here, Ollie thought. When Bo had suggested that they drive to Bornholm, she'd immediately agreed, as she always took every opportunity she could to see more of the region in which she was working.

With little Mat in his pram, she had explored Copenhagen's many tourist attractions. She'd visited its stunning museums, ambled its streets and taken a harbour tour, and Bo had also taken the time to show her the hidden-away gems of the city he called his home. They'd also made trips to Dragor. She'd adored its narrow streets and low houses built in the eighteenth and nineteenth centuries, and had been entranced by its old port. They'd also visited the cultural harbour city of Helsingør and Ollie had explored Kronberg Castle. There was so much of the country to see but she was out of time.

She had just ten days left in Denmark and, every time she thought about getting on a plane and returning home, her stomach filled with acid-covered concrete. But she had to leave, she couldn't stay.

Stupidly, she'd been living in a fool's paradise since she'd started sleeping with Bo, pretending that the idyll they'd created would last—her looking after Mat and him going off to work, coming home at night to spend time with his son before turning his attention to loving her. Nothing lasted and Ollie tried to remind herself that she preferred it that way.

She wasn't convinced.

The truth was that she was a hair's breadth away from falling in love with Bo, with Mat, with Copenhagen and with this amazing country. Their holiday in Bornholm would be the last bit of concentrated time they'd spend with each other, and three days after they returned to the city she would catch a flight to London.

Staying with Bo was not an option.

Ollie looked down when her phone vibrated. She'd taken a photo of Gundjem shortly after leaving the car and posted it on the Cooper family's group. Her mum's reply was a picture of Ollie's empty but decorated office at Cooper & Co complete with its state-of-the-art computer and a framed copy of her degree on the wall.

Standing there, overlooking Gundjem and watching the fishing boats coming into the harbour, with Bo's arms around her, Ollie knew with absolute certainty that she didn't want to join the family firm or to go back to London. She'd thought she could do the job for five years, that it was something she could do with some gritting of her teeth. She now knew she couldn't. Not now and not at any time in the future.

It wasn't an office job she was allergic to—if she joined Sabine it would mean she could mostly work remotely. But working with figures and company law in a fast-paced, corporate environment would sap her and make her miserable.

She wanted to be here, with Bo and Mat, living with them, loving them. But, even if they weren't part of her future, given Bo had made it clear that she couldn't expect a long-term commitment from him, she still wanted to buy a share in Sabine's business. She wanted to learn from her as she supplied au pairs and nannies to good families who needed their help and input.

She'd made a promise to her parents, and that was important to her. At the very, very least, she needed to have a sensible, reasonable discussion about how she could fulfil her obligations without selling her soul and drowning in misery.

She knew, standing here on Denmark's sunshine island, that she couldn't be a part of Cooper & Co and somehow she and her family would have to come to terms with that. She was going to be without the man she loved—she knew that Bo would not change his mind and ask her to stay—but five years was far too long to spend time not doing what she loved. It was too long to be without the people she loved, but she didn't have a choice in that. She did with her career.

'You're a million miles away,' Bo said, his mouth close to her ear. She jumped a little and squeezed his forearm. She turned in his arms and tipped her head back to look at him, trying to burn all the details of this moment into her brain. Bo was dressed in a button-down navy-and-white-striped shirt with the sleeves rolled up, blue shorts and boat shoes, his hair blowing in the warm wind. His eyes crinkled at the corners as he smiled down at her, and she loved the fact that he hadn't shaved for a day or two. His stubble made him look a little more devil-may-care, a lot more disreputable. More like a sailor than the owner of one of the continent's premier boat-building yards and an amazing yacht designer.

Over the past few weeks, she'd come to know the man behind the reserved facade he showed the world. He had a dry sense of humour and a fondness for the ridiculous and, now that he was used to it, enjoyed her gentle teasing. He was considerate, occasionally affectionate and, if he sometimes spent far too much time on his drawing boards or on his laptop in a world of his own, she let him be, understanding that he was in his happy place, zoned out on water displacement, bows, masts and drag.

But sometimes he'd look up from working on his laptop, see her sitting on the couch reading or watching a movie and hand her a warm smile, as if to say 'hey, you're still here and that's pretty damn marvellous'. He'd started singing folk songs to Mat after reading to him and, when she'd asked him what he was singing, he'd told her they were songs his grandmother had sung to him when he was a young boy. She was glad that he'd reconnected with music and enjoyed his baritone. It was an improvement on the out-of-tune eighties rock tunes she belted out that caused the neighbourhood cats to flee and Mat to slap his hands over his ears.

Bo lifted his hand and dragged his thumb over her bottom lip. 'You are so very beautiful, Olivia,' he murmured, and Ollie saw the sincerity in his eyes. He'd told her she was lovely before, but she couldn't wrap her head around the fact that such a gorgeous guy thought she was hot.

She just wished he could think of her as something more than a blip on his radar, someone who was worth more than an eight-week affair. But while she could speak to her parents, rearrange her work priorities, change her career and flip things around in her own life, she could not influence his.

She couldn't make him love her, she couldn't make him commit. She didn't have the power to grant him the ability to trust or to take a risk. She was just a girl who was lucky to have shared his life for as long as she had.

But, damn, saying goodbye, leaving, was going to be the mental equivalent of being flayed with a whip.

CHAPTER TWELVE

IN FRONT OF the floor-to-ceiling window that overlooked the bleach-white beach and glistening sea, Bo looked down into Ollie's lovely eyes and lifted his hands to cradle her face. She looked ethereal in the pale light flowing in from the yet-to-set sun. From the moment he'd first seen her just shy of two months ago, he'd visualised making love to her here, in the bedroom of his island home. He'd wanted to see the evening light on her skin, watch her eyes fog over as the water smacked the beach below the house, breathing in the air coming off the sea as he painted his desire on her glorious skin.

Ever so slowly, wanting to take his time, desperate to make a memory, Bo undid the neck-to-hem buttons of her pretty, short sundress, eventually spreading it open to reveal her lacy, mint-green bra and high-cut matching panties. He dragged his finger down the centre of her chest and watched her nipples pebble, hardening in anticipation of how he would make her feel.

Oh, he intended to make her feel....*everything*.

Lifting his hand, he gripped the clip that held her soft curls against the back of her head and let the heavy mass fall down her back, over her slim shoulders. Ollie lifted her chin and parted her lips, and he knew she wanted him to kiss her. But if he lost himself in her mouth this would be over far too soon. Avoiding her mouth, he dragged his lips over her jaw, before tugging her ear lobe into his mouth. She reached for him, but he shook his head, tipping her head back so that he could look into her deep-brown, glowing eyes.

'I need to explore you softly, slowly, intensely.'

He saw the tremble in her fingers, the way her skin pebbled in response to his words. He knew he turned her on—he was old enough and experienced enough to have worked that out weeks ago—but he doubted she knew how she affected him. She walked into the room and a barrage of images hit him: how he'd like to take her by that window, on that table. Time after time, his knees weakened and the air in the room seemed to evaporate. The urge to cover her mouth with his, whether they were in company or alone, was always present.

There had never been anyone in his life who made him lose his head so thoroughly; who could, with one look or one word, penetrate his carefully constructed armour. Ollie *got* him in a way that no one ever had. She knew more of him, of who he was and what he stood for, than anyone ever had before.

And, in just over a week, she would be leaving his life for ever. What would he do with Mat? Could he cope on his own? He didn't want her to go, but he knew she couldn't stay. She had promises to keep, a life to establish elsewhere.

Bo pushed those thoughts aside; they were for later. Right now, his only job was to love Ollie as thoroughly as he could. Pushing her dress off her shoulders, he led her over to the bed and sat down on the edge, pulling her between his legs. He rested his forehead on her sternum, inhaling her fresh air and jasmine scent, his lips resting on her lovely skin, his hands on her shapely hips.

Hooking one finger under the cup of her bra, he pulled it down and blew on her puckered nipple. Above his head, Ollie sighed and rested her hands on his shoulders, moving them to his hair and down his neck. He knew she wanted to touch him but also seemed to understand that something else was happening this evening, something bigger, bolder and brighter than their previous couplings.

Something important...

He didn't know if he loved her. Bo didn't know, with his family history, whether he was capable of loving anyone. But he couldn't deny that with Ollie he was close, as near to that elusive emotion they called love as he thought he could get. But it wasn't enough. He couldn't give Ollie all that she needed, everything she deserved.

But he could love her with his body, worship her with his lips, tongue and hands.

Bo reached behind her, undid the clasp holding her bra together and gently pulled the sexy garment from her body. When it landed on the floor, he covered her breast with his hands, his thumbs dragging across her nipples, making them tighter and harder. Knowing what she needed, he pulled one nipple into his mouth, sucking hard before pulling away to love the other. She was beautiful and tonight, for the next week, she was his. He'd take these long summer days, the few they'd been gifted, and he'd love her as best as he could, as much as he could.

At the end of it, he'd face his and Mat's Ollie-free future.

The thought made him want to howl, and then break things.

Bo gave himself a mental kick and told himself to concentrate. He had a gorgeous woman in his arms; he should give her, and her body, all the attention it deserved. And that meant running his lips over her ribs, dipping his tongue into her cute, ring-studded belly button. She had a tattoo of a swallow on her hip, pretty and perfect.

Bo dragged her panties down her hips and, when she stepped out of them, he stood up and told her to sit on the edge of the bed. Feeling hot, he stripped off to his briefs and sank to his knees between Ollie's thighs, smiling a little when her mouth dropped into a perfect 'O'.

He'd kissed her intimately a few times before, but he'd never made her orgasm with his fingers and tongue—he'd always been so desperate to be inside her.

Not being inside her when she came might kill

him but certain things were worth losing his life for...

Bo lay next to Ollie and watched the aftermath of her intense orgasm, feeling as if he'd conquered Everest and rowed across the Southern Ocean. He was an experienced lover, but nothing was more important than her being fully satisfied. Bo watched as she opened her intensely dark eyes, smiled and reached for him.

'That was a very one-sided couple of minutes, Sørenson,' she whispered as his hand encircled her, her thumb moving slowly across his tip. 'How do you want it? How do you want me?'

He mentally flipped through a couple of positions, discounted them all and settled for covering her slim body with his, hooking her legs over his hips. There was nothing exotic about the missionary position but it allowed them to be face to face, eye to eye, and he could watch her lovely face as passion spun him away.

Bo pushed inside her and sighed. She felt like home, the person he didn't think he'd been looking for. He didn't know how he was going to let her go but neither could he ask her to stay.

Ollie sat on the beach below Bo's house and watched Bo walk along the shoreline with Mat on his hip. He wore a pair of low-slung swimming shorts and a navy chambray shirt half-buttoned up. His big feet left an impression in the wet sand and he was chatting to Mat, who seemed to find his father extraordinarily funny.

Mat and Bo had bonded, and Bo was now confident in his ability to look after his son. For Ollie, time was running out and she was deeply concerned that Bo didn't have someone to take her place as a nanny when she left. Greta had agreed to help Bo out temporarily but Bo using his housekeeper as Mat's nanny, as wonderful as Greta was, was not a long-term solution.

This afternoon, while Mat took his nap, she intended to make Bo read the CVs of the five nannies she and Sabine had decided were good enough for Bo to interview. Despite Bo's lack of interest in the process, she couldn't, *wouldn't*, leave them without a solid back-up plan. It was going to be hard enough to leave but leaving Bo without a nanny to back him up would be an additional stress. Oh, she knew that Bo would cope—he could deal with anything and everything life tossed him—but she knew that being a single parent was taxing. He couldn't run a successful company and give Mat the time and attention he needed without some help. If she couldn't stay, then she wanted him to have a sensible, strong, loving person to look after Mat when Bo had to work.

She so wanted to stay. Ollie placed her hand on her heart, cursing herself for becoming so involved in this little family. She'd promised herself that she wouldn't become attached, but here she was, the human equivalent of a barnacle. She loved Mat and she was probably, *definitely*, in love with Bo.

And she had to leave.

Last night, after lying awake in Bo's arms, she'd considered her options, one of which was taking out a business loan to buy shares in Sabine's business. If she managed to secure a loan, then she could split her savings between paying back her parents some of the money they'd spent on her education—it was all she could think to do or offer—servicing the loan repayments and putting a little towards establishing a new life in Paris. But was Paris where she wanted to live? Was London?

If she couldn't have Copenhagen—and she couldn't—where could she see herself living?

She could live in any European city: most of her work would be online. She'd run through a dozen cities last night, finding something, or a few things, wrong with all of them. After getting into a total tizz, she'd reminded herself that she had a couple of hurdles to negotiate—she needed to talk to her parents, secure the loan and make Sabine a formal offer— before she needed to make such a big decision.

She knew that Copenhagen would always be top of her list. But having her around full-time wasn't something Bo wanted. She was a temporary fling, on her way out. That made Bo sound callous and selfish, when he wasn't. He enjoyed her company, was a kind, considerate and thoughtful house mate, a clear-headed and calm boss and a blow-her-socks-off lover—but he'd never hinted, not once, that he wanted her to stay.

And if he did, she couldn't, not the way things

were now. She needed a lot, *lot* more from Bo before she could consider staying in Copenhagen: love, trust, some sort of commitment. She needed everything that Bo couldn't give her.

Her phone jangled in her back pocket and Ollie pulled it out, grateful for the reprieve. She saw Helen's name on the screen and pushed the green button, happy to hear from her good friend.

'Hey, you. Where are you?'

Helen's face appeared on the screen. It looked as though she was sitting at a dining-room table, with a painting behind her by Degas, depicting his beloved ballerinas. Knowing how wealthy Helen's employers were, it was probably an original.

Helen placed her chin in her hand. 'So, I have news. I think you know that my boys are getting big now—one is already at boarding school, and another is going to be starting soon. The youngest is only ten, but Adele wants to cut back at work, and she's planning on working from home more.'

Ollie wrinkled her nose. 'Are they letting you go?'

Helen nodded and Ollie winced. It was never easy to leave a family, especially when she'd been with them for such a long time. 'And how are you feeling about that?' she asked her friend.

Helen smiled. 'Better than they are, frankly! We had a long conversation last night and they were in tears. They don't want me to go but there won't be much for me to do. And they don't want me to think I've done anything wrong, because they adore me...'

Ollie smiled, happy for her friend and proud of the excellent relationship she had with her employers. 'The truth is, I need a change,' Helen admitted. 'That's why I'm calling…'

Ollie frowned, not understanding the expectant look on Helen's face. 'I fell in love with Copenhagen when I was there, and I wouldn't mind going back.'

'I'd love to have you, but I'm leaving in a week.' Ollie placed her hand on her heart, trying to rub the stabbing pain away.

'I'm hinting when I should just come out and say this. I want to interview for the position of little Mat's nanny, if it hasn't already been filled.'

It took a little time for Helen's words to make sense and, when they did, Ollie released a squeal of delight. 'Are you serious?'

If it were up to her, she'd employ Helen in a heartbeat. She was warm, funny, organised and had an affinity for children of all ages. She'd studied to be a teacher, but she was an exceptional nanny, the best Ollie had come across. There was no one she wanted to look after Mat more.

'Has the position been filled?' Helen asked, looking worried. 'Please tell me it's not been filled.'

Ollie looked to where Bo was and saw that he was walking back to her. 'No, it hasn't, mostly because my boss won't look at applications. Send me your CV and I will campaign hard to get him to employ you. I couldn't leave Mat in better hands, Helen.'

Helen tipped her head to the side. 'Then why do

I sense a note of un-enthusiasm in your voice? An "*I don't want to leave*"?'

Because she didn't. But she couldn't stay, and she couldn't let this situation continue as it was. She had decisions to make, conversations to have and hurdles to overcome. But Helen as Mat's nanny would be a weight off her mind.

'Send me your CV immediately and I'll put it in front of his nose,' Ollie told her, rushing her words. 'I was planning on pinning him down this afternoon anyway.'

'Sounds like fun.'

Ollie looked up and saw Bo standing a few feet from her, a naughty "*can't wait to have you*" look in his eyes. Yeah, that would be fun, but their conversation wouldn't be.

But it was time to face the music...

'I'll speak to you soon, Helen. Just send me that email quickly, yeah?'

Ollie disconnected the call and stood up, brushing sand off the seat of her denim shorts. Mat leaned towards her and Ollie took him from Bo, smiling when he wrapped his chubby legs around her and buried his face in her neck. The combination of sun, sand and sea had tired him out and she knew he'd be asleep before they reached the house. She turned her head to kiss Mat's head and watched Bo gather their towels, their beach basket and the cooler they'd brought down earlier that morning.

Bo looked at her, a slight smile on his face. 'Time to go home?'

Ollie nodded. Yes, it was time to go home. She just wished she didn't think that home was wherever he and Mat were.

After a quick shower, Ollie walked from the master suite into the study that adjoined the magnificent master study. Opening up Bo's computer, she logged into her email account and printed off the five CVs she wanted to show him, happy to add in Helen's.

They were going to have this conversation now, today. She wanted Bo and Mat to have the best nanny there was and that meant Helen needed to replace her when she left. She was even more highly in demand than Ollie and would be snapped up in a heartbeat if Bo didn't hire her immediately. He could not dilly-dally on this, he needed to act, and act immediately.

Having Helen looking after Mat would be a huge relief, and she wouldn't have to worry about whether Bo was coping, or how he was juggling being a full-time dad with being a busy CEO and yacht designer. Thank goodness that Mat was still so young while all these changes were happening in his life. If he'd been older, she'd have been a great deal more concerned about the number of caregivers he'd had in his life. But Helen was a stayer, and she would be there for five years, possibly a lot longer, a loving and stable influence in Mat's life. Between Bo and her, Mat would have all the love, support, discipline and care he needed.

The sad thing was that he'd never remember Ollie. Would Bo, in time, forget about her too? Would she be relegated to the outskirts of the mind, to that place where memories gradually faded? The reality was that, in a few months, she'd be a nice memory; in a few years, he wouldn't be able to recall her features.

Ollie sucked in a deep breath and cursed her burning eyes.

It is what it is, Olivia, you can't change it because you don't like it.

This was the price she was paying because, once again, despite knowing it wasn't a clever option or idea, she'd become attached.

She had no one to blame but herself.

Ollie walked down the long hallway of Bo's magnificent summer house, knowing that she would find Bo on the outside deck, the one that overlooked the private beach nestled between two rocky outcrops. He stood by the tempered-glass railing, a beer in his hand and the light wind lifting the strands of his hair. For as long as she lived, she'd remember him standing there, bare feet and looking relaxed, with the seascape behind him.

He sent her a slow smile and lifted his beer. 'Would you like one?'

She shook her head. A look of confusion crossed his face when, instead of walking over to him and curling herself into him as she normally did, she pulled out a dining chair at the handcrafted wooden table and gestured for him to join her. When he took a seat opposite her, he noticed the pile of papers on the table and groaned. 'It's too beautiful a day to be serious, Ol. Let's just enjoy our time together while Mat is asleep.'

Ollie wavered. She loved his little boy, but she'd come to crave those hours when she could lie in Bo's arms, discussing everything and nothing. They also spent a lot of their alone time making love but, while she was tempted—she was always tempted; Bo just did it for her!—she knew that they had to talk about the future. *Right now.* Helen wouldn't hang around waiting for Mr Picky to make up his mind.

Ollie put her hand on the CVs and sent Bo a serious look. 'You've been ignoring my and Sabine's requests to discuss my replacement for weeks now, and we can't put it off any longer.'

Bo lifted his beer bottle to his mouth and she saw the irritation in those green depths. He liked calling the shots and controlling the conversation but she wasn't going to allow him to do that today. This was too important to leave until the very last minute.

'Do you remember that I told you that I met my friend Helen in Copenhagen a couple of weeks back?' Ollie began. 'We met at a cafe in Tivoli Gardens.'

He lifted one shoulder. 'Vaguely.'

Of course he remembered; the man had a mind like a steel trap. He was just punishing her for pushing ahead with this conversation, for spoiling their time together by inviting reality to the party. Ollie narrowed her eyes in a warning he couldn't miss. He shrugged and rolled his finger in a gesture for her to continue.

'Helen is a hugely experienced nanny and a lovely, lovely person. She's been with the same family for a long time, nearly ten years, and it's time for her to move on. She's expressed an interest in being Mat's nanny and I think you'd be a fool if you didn't snap her up. Now. *Today.*'

'I'm not ready to decide on a new nanny for Mat,' Bo said, looking obstinate.

'Bo, I am leaving soon. If you employ Helen today, she could give her family two weeks' notice—they love her and would allow her to go, knowing that she's needed—and you'll have somebody to help you out a lot sooner than I thought. You can't look after Mat and run your business.'

'I'll have Greta to help me.'

'Greta has her own life; she is not a long-term solution. Why are you burying your head in the sand?' she demanded. 'It's not like you, Bo.'

Bo pushed his chair back from the table so hard that it toppled over as he stood up. He stomped back over to the railing and gripped the edge, straightened his arms and looked down.

Ollie followed him to where he stood and placed a hand on his back. 'What's going on, Bo?'

'I need you to stay here, Ol.'

Damn. 'You know I can't do that, Bo. It's not possible.'

He stood up straight and folded his arms, looking like an annoyed Viking chief. 'You can. Just tell your parents you don't want to be an accountant and tell

Sabine that you aren't interested in buying a share in her business. Stay in Copenhagen with me and Mat.'

She could not possibly be hearing him correctly. Had he just dismissed her concerns about her family, brushed off her ambitions and demanded that she give up everything important to her to stay in her position as Mat's nanny?

Ollie frowned at him, unable to believe he could be so glib and dismissive. This wasn't the Bo she'd come to know and adore.

Ollie hauled in a deep breath and tried to hold onto her slipping temper. 'From the beginning, I told you I could only give you two months, Bo. You knew that. Look, I'm going to tell my parents I won't be joining their firm, and I'm going to offer to compensate them for the cost of my studies.'

'I'll pay them. How much is it? I can do the bank transfer today.'

He did not just say that! Ollie blinked and waited for him to apologise or to take back his words. He did neither. What was going on here?

'And how do I pay you back?' Ollie asked, increasingly annoyed by his high-handedness and arrogance. He was being a typical, bolshie alpha male, demanding and commanding.

'You can work it off,' he shot back.

By looking after Mat or by sleeping with him? Maybe her anger was clouding her judgement, but she was furious at his blithe dismissal of her feelings and her predicament. He simply wanted to throw his money at her to get the result he wanted. He had an excellent nanny to look after Mat and a willing bed partner and he didn't want to be inconvenienced. The arrogant jerk!

'I will never let you pay off my debts for me,' Ollie told him, ice coating her words. 'And as great as you are in bed, and as much as I love Mat, I have my own life to lead and goals to meet. I need more than this, Bo.'

And at that moment she did. Oh, she'd been happy being a nanny, but Ollie knew that it wasn't something she could do for the next five or ten years. While she didn't want to be an accountant, she did want to go into business. And, on the plus side, her accountancy degree would come in handy when it came to tax season.

Bo shoved the fingers of both hands into his hair. 'What's wrong with what we are doing now?'

How could he even ask her that? 'What's wrong with it is that it's all about me working for you, Bo! I can't spend the next few months or years looking after your kid during the day and warming your bed at night! Do you not see that?'

'You love being with Mat and me!'

She did, of course she did, but it wasn't enough, not long term. Even if Bo told her he loved her, she still didn't think being his partner and Mat's mum would be enough. She had a good brain, and she wanted to do more and be more. She wanted to be able to test her wings and try to fly.

She couldn't sacrifice her goals and ambitions because Bo wasn't a fan of change and because having

her around made life easy for him. She loved him...
but she loved herself too.

'I need to be more, do more, have more.'

His eyes sharpened and he slid his hands into the
pockets of his shorts. 'I suppose you are going to tell
me that you want more from me, from *us*. That you
aren't going to stay here without a ring on your finger and without me telling you that I love you and
that I can't live without you?'

His words were so scathing, and his eyes were so
cold that Ollie felt her bottom lip wobble. She would
not cry, damn it! She lifted her chin and pushed steel
into her spine. She was a Cooper, and they did not
buckle.

'My contract is ending,' she told him, trying to
hold onto her temper. 'You need a nanny. I have
found someone brilliant for you. I hope you employ
her because, if you don't, you'll regret it.

'I am doing what I always said I would and that's
moving on,' Ollie continued. 'You might not like
it—'

'And you do? Like it?' he interrupted. 'Then why
do you look like you are about to cry?'

He knew why—he knew that she loved him, that
she wanted more—but she refused to utter any words
she couldn't take back. She wouldn't admit that she'd
allowed herself to become attached to Mat and him.
Telling him that she loved him and not hearing the
words back would emotionally eviscerate her.

She was hurting enough as it was. Before today,
she'd harboured a small hope that he might love her,

that he might come out and admit there might be a future for them, but his cold speech had destroyed any lingering dreams she still had.

He didn't love her, was never going to love her, and probably *couldn't* love her.

And damn him for noticing the tears she refused to let fall.

She wasn't going to explain herself and it was time to walk away. She still had several days left in his company, and she needed to be professional, so saying anything else that would raise the temperature between them wasn't an option. As it was, they were surface-of-the-sun hot.

Ollie stomped back over to the table, picked up the thin stack of papers and slapped the pile against his chest. Because he was stubborn, the CVs fluttered to the deck and Ollie was damned if she was going to pick them up. 'Hire a nanny, Sørenson.'

Spinning round, she walked away from Bo, her tears creating pools of acid in her eyes and her throat.

CHAPTER THIRTEEN

Bo LOOKED AT Ollie's straight, taut back and silently cursed. He'd suspected for a while now that Ollie had feelings for him that went beyond the bedroom, and that he meant more to her than a quick fling with her boss.

It was in her warm eyes, in the way she looked at him and sighed. He could see it when her face softened and in her many, sometimes subconscious, gestures of affection: a head on his shoulder here, a hand on his knee there. Despite her vow not to become attached again, she had—with Mat and with him.

She loved Mat, of that he had no doubt. She might even be in love with him...

And he was halfway to being in love with her... but it wasn't enough. Love never was.

Honestly, it would be easy to tell her that he had feelings for her—it was the truth—and to ask her to stay. He could see them living together, being together, raising Mat and any other kids they had together. Her staying in Copenhagen with him would be an elegant solution to some of his current problems.

But…

But she wanted more than to be a wife and mother, she wanted her own business, to make her mark on the world. Deep down inside, he knew she wasn't being unreasonable, and could admit he was being ridiculously unfair by asking her to make Mat and him her entire focus, but he felt the need to push the envelope. He wanted to test whether she'd make the sacrifices for him his parents never had. He wanted her to prove that she wasn't anything like his mother, to show him over and over again that his heart, and Mat's, would be in super-safe hands.

But, in doing that, wasn't he emulating his father, placing what he needed and wanted above what his wife and son needed? He was a product of two dysfunctional people and today he was showing Ollie exactly how messed up he truly was.

But he couldn't stop. If he did, he would have to slice himself open emotionally and allow her to take full possession of his heart, to trust that she wouldn't hurt him.

He couldn't do it. It was too much of a risk, and he knew that any hope and optimism—love—were being obliterated by fear, old hurts and the reopening of ancient wounds.

'You can't have it all, Ollie,' he said, halting her progress off the deck.

He watched as she turned round and walked back to him, her back ramrod-straight and her eyes narrowed.

'What do you mean by that?'

'You can't be a wife and a mother and a lover. Not with me, at least.'

He knew that his words would be a death blow, killing whatever they'd had. He also knew that Ollie would never stand for the ultimatum he was laying down, but wasn't killing this quickly better than death by degrees? In the long run, wouldn't this hurt less?

'What are you trying to say, Bo?' she asked, genuinely confused.

'You've been imagining us being together, that we could commit to each other and raise Mat together,' he said, pushing the words out. Man, this was more painful than he'd thought it would be. When she didn't issue a denial, he sighed and pushed on. 'If you stayed, you would have to choose between me and having a business, and we'd have to be your only priority.'

She looked at him for a long time before speaking again. 'So, you are asking me to stay here with you as your lover? And nanny to Mat?'

Ollie blinked, waiting for him to say something else. He frowned, wondering what was going on in her sharp brain and behind her now cool eyes.

'For interest's sake, what do I get if I agree to that, Bo?'

Because he'd never imagined that this conversation would get this far, he had to think quickly. He shrugged and gestured to his house. 'You'd get to live in one of the most beautiful countries in the world, in one of the most exciting capitals on the planet and stay in spectacular houses. You and Mat would travel with me, five star all the way. I'd give you a generous allowance and…'

Her instruction to stop talking wasn't loud but he heard it. He searched her face for what she was feeling but, for the first time, he couldn't read her and knew he'd gone too far. She was a blank canvas, remote and impenetrable. 'No.'

Right, well, there it was—finally. Although he'd expected her to refuse his offer, he still felt wildly disappointed.

She looked past his shoulder to the sea beyond him and he watched her shoulders rise and fall. When she looked back at him, he saw the disappointment in her eyes. 'You made that offer knowing that I would never agree to it and it was beneath you.'

Maybe.

'The sad thing is, you have no idea what I want and need from you—even less than my ex-fiancé, and that's saying something. Or any man.'

'And what's that?'

'Your unquestionable support. I'd need you to hand me a set of wings and tell me to fly, to tell me that'll you'll catch me if I fall. I'd need you to love me enough to allow me to reach my full potential as a person.

'I'm worth that, Bo. And, if you can't see that, if you can't give that to me, then it's right that I walk away…just as you intended me to.'

Anger, pain and disappointment chased each other across her face and a cold hand squeezed his heart.

He'd hurt her and he hadn't wanted to do that. But he knew that, if someone tried to be everything, they ended up failing somewhere down the line and people got hurt.

Ollie tipped her head and narrowed her eyes at him. 'Here's a counter-offer for you: why don't you stay at home full-time and look after Mat? You have lots of money and I doubt you'd need to work again if you didn't have to. Why don't you give up work and look after Mat full-time? Then I'll run my business.'

Give up designing? Walk away from Sørenson Yachts? Was she mad? Before he could tell her how ludicrous her suggestion was, she lifted her eyebrows. 'I can see the "no" all over your face. So, tell me, why is there a set of rules for you but they don't apply to me? Why is your professional fulfilment so much more important than mine?'

Bo rubbed the back of his neck. Of course it wasn't and he had no defence. So he dug his hole a little deeper when he spoke again. 'I design yachts and you look after kids for a living—it's not the same!'

'Of course it is!' Ollie whipped back. 'That is such a weak argument, Sørenson!'

Ollie held up her hand. 'Look, we're going around in circles. I want it all, Bo, and you can't give me that. You know it and I know it. So I am going to make this easy on both of us and walk away from you and Mat as you very obviously want me to do. I survived Becca's death, and I'll survive losing you and Mat too. It'll hurt, but I will be okay.'

She pushed her curls off her face and tried to smile. 'Was I an idiot for becoming attached to you? Sure. I knew that it would end like this. But I'd rather be an idiot who had two wonderful months with you than be careful and miss out. I'd rather be an idiot who's prepared to take a chance on love and being hurt than living in the past and being too scared to step outside his comfort zone.'

Right, it was obvious he was the idiot.

Ollie looked down at the papers lying at their feet before allowing her eyes to connect with his. 'Hire Helen, Bo. You won't regret it, I promise you.'

'Love.'

It was such a small word, just four letters, but it had the power to make or break a person's spirit, to buoy them up or to make them plummet down into the depths of hell.

Bo felt plenty of other 'L' words for her—like and lust came to mind. Love was not one of them. If he did, he would want what was best for her, he'd want her to be everything she could be with no restrictions. If he loved her, he would trust her to make good decisions, for herself and them, the family she so desperately wanted with him. He'd want her to be more, do more and achieve more than just being his nanny-cum-lover.

Ollie loved her job—it was an honour and a responsibility looking after someone else's child—but, damn it, she was allowed to want more, to be more. She was allowed to have a career, as well as be a parent and a lover. To love and be loved. As her parents' marriage had shown her, two strong, successful people could have it all.

She understood why Bo thought it wasn't possible. He had a terrible relationship with Bridget, and had not had much of a relationship with his father. His mother's primary focus had been, and still was, on her work. She'd never given her husband or son any emotional support or showed any interest in them as people, in their lives or in their interests.

But, man, it hurt that Bo was confusing her with his fridge-for-a-heart mother. Ollie knew about boundaries and was emotionally aware enough to lead a balanced life—she'd watched her mum do it all her life. Her mum worked full-time but neither she nor her brothers had felt as if they were emotionally neglected. Her parents had always made sure that they were home at a reasonable hour, they'd eaten dinner together as a family and weekends had been declared work-free zones. They'd been present, interested and involved. Apart from their disagreement about her choice of career, they'd been pretty awesome parents.

But it was her career, her life, and she wouldn't let Bo or her parents tell her how to live it. Becca's death had taught her that she didn't know how much time she had on this rock called Earth and she wasn't going to waste any of it.

She'd find a way around her parents' expectations; it required her to have a tough conversation with them but she was up for that. She should've addressed this issue a long time ago but, feeling numb from Becca's death, she'd simply pushed it away and shoved her head into the sand. After her hard conversation with Bo two days ago, she felt she was strong enough to tackle her parents. After all, her heart was broken already.

Standing on the beach, Ollie looked up at the house above her, thinking of the man inside who would be waking up around now. She'd slipped out of the house much earlier, unable to sleep in the guest bedroom alone.

Their relationship had shifted seismically and the words they'd said couldn't be pulled back. She'd been too hurt and angry to sleep with, or even talk to him, so she'd removed her clothes from Bo's closet and her toiletries from his bathroom and decamped to the luxurious guest bedroom, the one furthest from his.

She was now his son's nanny, nothing more and nothing less. The baby monitor in her hand vibrated and she turned up the volume. Through the state-of-the-art speaker, she heard Mat's snuffle and knew it was time to head back to the house. She was exhausted, emotionally wiped out, and was operating on minimal sleep. She didn't know how she was going to get through the day.

But she would. She had a job to do and money to earn.

'Hello, my beautiful boy.'

Ollie heard Bo's voice on the baby monitor and placed her hand on her heart. She sank to the sand and placed her head on her knees as she listened to her lover tell his son how amazing he was and how much he loved him.

She heard the sound of Mat's baby grow being unsnapped, the crackle of a nappy being laid out and Mat's gurgling laughter as Bo blew raspberries on his fat tummy. It was what Bo did every time he changed Mat's nappy.

Bo was madly, crazy, head-over-heels in love with Mat. She just wished he felt the same way about her.

But if wishes were horses and all that... He didn't love her, he couldn't commit to her and she should get used to the fact.

'So, this morning I spoke to a lovely lady who wants to meet you again,' Bo told Mat. 'I interviewed her, and she sounds amazing, and I think you'll like her. And, best of all, she'll be a nanny and only a nanny. I won't be distracted again.'

Helen? It had to be...

'I told her that I needed her urgently and she's agreed to be here by the end of the week.'

Mat released another stream of babble and Ollie imagined he was telling his dad that nobody was as wonderful as Ollie and that he'd miss her. It was far more likely that the little boy was probably just asking for his breakfast.

'I'm going to miss her too, but we can't find a middle ground.'

Ollie frowned at the baby monitor. What? He hadn't offered her a middle ground! It had been his way or no way—'stay here and don't do or be anything else'.

Ollie resisted the urge to storm up to the house and set him straight. But she didn't have the energy and her heart had been kicked around enough as it was. Bo had drawn his line in the sand and that was as far and as deep as he wanted to go.

It wasn't deep enough and far enough for her. Knowing she couldn't listen any more, Ollie switched off the baby monitor and allowed the tears to trickle down her face.

Bo was with Mat, and she could take a few more minutes to sit on the private beach on this special island. It was, Ollie admitted, a spectacularly pretty place to get heartbroken.

Well done, Ollie.

In the end, their parting was terribly civil and very mature. It was everything Ollie didn't feel. Helen had arrived in Copenhagen when they returned from Bornholm, and Ollie had helped Helen move into the second of Bo's very luxurious guest bedrooms and and had taken her through Mat's routine.

Mat, being the sunny character he was, had gurgled and laughed his way through the transition, happy to spend the majority of his time in Helen's arms. With Bo avoiding her, or only talking to her when he absolutely had to, Ollie had felt as if he'd pushed her to the side, a spare part for a well-tuned car.

But her immense sadness at leaving Bo and Mat had been tempered by relief as she couldn't live with the implacable and reticent Bo any longer. She hardly recognised the man she'd loved and laughed with, the one who'd loved her so thoroughly, who'd looked at her with affection and who'd bestowed his sweet, slow smiles on her.

On the morning she was due to fly out, Ollie promised herself she wouldn't cry. But tears burned her eyes when she hugged Mat for the last time, and her heart cracked when Helen kissed her cheek, hugged her and walked Mat back into Bo's house, leaving Bo and her alone outside. Bo placed her luggage in the taxi and, when he came back to stand in front of her, she couldn't meet his eyes, choosing to stare at the walnut-brown sweater covering his wide chest.

'I'm sorry I can't give you what you need, Olivia,' Bo said as he opened the door to the taxi for her.

She tipped her head back to look at him, taking in the two-day-old stubble on his hard jaw, the furrow between his eyebrows and his taut mouth. 'Do you even know what I need, Bo?'

Confusion jumped into his eyes, and she knew that he didn't get it. Or, if he did, he didn't want to acknowledge the truth. She considered getting into the taxi and leaving, but she didn't want to leave with misunderstandings between them.

Gathering her courage, she looked into those eyes she loved so much and forced her tongue to form the words she needed to say and he needed to hear. 'I love you and I want to be with you. I want to help you raise Mat. But I also want to work, to do something worthwhile and important. I wish you could trust me when I tell you that I wouldn't hurt you or Mat, Bo.'

He looked as though an invisible pair of hands was around his neck and squeezing tight. 'You're asking me to take too big a chance, Olivia, a massive risk. And I can't.'

She nodded, blinking back her tears. 'I guess I knew that but I had to try.' Knowing that there was nothing more to say, she stood on her tiptoes and kissed his cheek, inhaling his fresh, clean, citrusy aftershave for the last time. 'Goodbye, Bo. Hug your boy every day for me.'

Ollie slipped into the back seat, shut the door, rested her head on the headrest and closed her eyes.

It was done. Her Copenhagen caper was over. Now she just had to find a way to live her life without Bo and Mat in it.

CHAPTER FOURTEEN

OLLIE'S PARENTS HAD a strict dress code for all their employees—suit and tie for the men, corporate boring for the women—and Ollie knew that arriving in tight, skinny jeans, an off-the-shoulder top and high-top trainers was not suitable corporate attire. She saw eyebrows rising as she walked down the long hallway of Cooper & Co, trying to ignore the pointed glances of her parents' employees behind the glass-walled offices.

Taking a deep breath, she walked to the end of the hallway where her parents and two of her brothers had their offices, and looked to the left at the empty office she knew had been designated for her use. She shook her head. Nope, not happening. Her office was next to her oldest brother's and, feeling her eyes on him, Michael lifted his head and grinned. Then his grin faded, and he grimaced as he looked to the conference room behind her.

A talk with their parents in the conference room was never a good thing. He mouthed, 'Are you okay?' and Ollie responded by rocking her hand up and down.

She would be; she just had to get through the next half hour. It wasn't going to be fun in any way.

Through the glass walls of the swish conference room, Ollie watched her parents walk out of the massive office they shared. They'd managed to live and work together for so many years and it amazed her. Her father was tall and dignified. Her mum was shorter and rounder but, as always, was immaculately dressed. Energy crackled off her. Her mum could work, raise kids, be the chair of the PTA and bake bread. She was a master at multitasking and, because of her, Ollie knew that she could be a wife, a lover, a mother and a businesswoman.

But it didn't matter what she *knew* she could do. Bo had needed to be convinced and that hadn't happened. That wouldn't happen.

She missed him. Since leaving Copenhagen three days ago, she hadn't heard from him. Helen had sent her a couple of messages and photos of Mat, and he seemed fine, as happy and wonderful as always. Helen hadn't mentioned Bo and Ollie hadn't asked.

Her phone remained stupidly, stubbornly silent and Ollie cursed herself for thinking that he would message or call, or that he would follow her to London. She was spinning impossible dreams and she pushed those thoughts away. He'd made his position clear—he couldn't, wouldn't, commit to her. He wouldn't commit to anyone, ever. She would never hear from him again and it was time to start accepting that reality.

But it hurt so much. She felt as if she were walking around with a heart punctured by porcupine quills. And that the quills were still lodged in her barely functioning organ.

The door to the conference room opened and her father stepped back to let her mum precede him. Her dad had beautiful manners and, despite being a force of nature herself and a feminist to the core, her mum loved her dad's courtly gestures.

Ollie crossed the room to him, allowing his strong arms to come around her, resting her head on his strong chest. Her dad gave the best hugs and she wished that she didn't have to disappoint him.

But she couldn't live a lie. Nor could she spend the next five years hating every minute of her job and life.

Her mum looked at her watch and cleared her throat. 'We have a busy day and need to get on,' she told Ollie, and then raised her eyebrows at her super-casual outfit. 'That's not how I expect you to dress at work, Olivia.'

'But I'm not one of your employees, Mum,' Ollie said, pulling out a chair and sitting down. And she never would be. Her parents just didn't know it yet.

After her parents were seated, her mum directly opposite her and her dad one chair to the right, Ollie gathered her courage. She just needed to spit it out and be done.

Expect fireworks, expect recriminations, and maybe some raised voices, but you can't let that put you off.

She was convinced that they could find a solution that wouldn't involve her sacrificing the next five years of her life.

'I came here to talk to you about the fact that I am supposed to start work here in ten days,' Ollie said.

Jasmine leaned forward and tapped her bright-pink nails on the glass table. 'Olivia, please don't tell me you are taking another nannying position. We made a deal that you would return to work.'

Ollie shook her head. 'I can't do it, Mum, please don't ask me to.' Ollie hauled in a deep breath before continuing. 'I understand that you spent an enormous amount of money on my education, and I am prepared to pay you back. I can do a transfer this afternoon, and maybe we could work out a payment plan, with interest, for me to repay you the rest over a couple of years.'

Her mum looked as though she'd been hit with a thick branch of a tree. Her father, strangely, didn't look that surprised. He simply leaned back, folded his arms across his chest and sent her an easy smile.

'We never expected you to repay us the money, Olivia, and I'm sorry if you felt like there were conditions attached to us educating you. That was our choice and our pleasure. We know that you love what you do, but you can be more than a nanny. It's a fine job, I'm not knocking it, but you have a first-class brain and we'd like to see you use it in a more—' he hesitated '—business-like setting. But, if being a nanny is what you have your heart set on, then we will support you.'

He frowned at her mum, who was staring down

at her nails. Paul cleared his throat, and her mum finally lifted her head and nodded.

It was a huge concession and Ollie knew how lucky she was to have parents who loved her beyond reason.

'I'm still not happy about you not joining our firm,' Jasmine told her, lifting her chin. 'You'd earn a huge salary and all the perks that come with a corporate job.'

'What makes you think I don't have that now?' Ollie asked. 'I earn a very good salary, Mum!'

'You earn a good wage, darling—professionals earn salaries,' her mum snapped back.

Sighing, Ollie tapped her phone, pulled up her latest wage slip and pushed her phone across the table. Her father grinned when he saw her take-home pay and a touch of pink touched her cheeks. Right, that should shut her mum up for a minute—maybe two.

'So what's the plan, Olivia?' her dad asked her.

'Why do you think I have a plan?' Ollie asked him, surprised at his perspicacity. If still waters ran deep, then her dad was a mile-deep aquifer.

'Because we didn't raise a fool. You've always had a plan—you've always thought ahead. So, what is it?'

She shrugged. She might as well tell them. 'I want to buy into Sabine's nanny business. If you are being serious about me not needing to repay you for the cost of my education—'

'We are,' her dad assured her.

She sent him a grateful, tremulous smile. 'Then I can buy a quarter-share of her business. It will take me a while but I will eventually, hopefully, buy her out.'

Paul nodded and scratched his chin. 'Right. And how much would you need to buy this business?' he asked.

Ollie told him the figure and waited for him to flinch. When he didn't, she was reminded that her father dealt with huge figures and numbers all the time. 'Ask her to send me her financials: I want to do a deep-dive into her books. I'm not letting my daughter buy into a company if I haven't inspected the company financials.'

It took all of Ollie's willpower not to fling herself across the table and hug her dad. Instead, she sent him another tremulous smile and blinked away her tears. He *got* her. He sent her a small wink and spoke again.

'And you won't be buying a small share. With what you have to spend, you could buy half her business,' Paul added.

Ollie stared at her dad, wondering if this was the moment when he'd lost the plot. She spread her hands out. She didn't have that sort of money. 'Dad, what are you talking about?'

He smiled at her. 'I received an email from a Bo Sørenson earlier this week.'

Bo? Her Bo? What was happening here?

'He transferred a hundred thousand pounds into our trust account, with explicit instructions that the money was to be used any way you wanted to. He explained the money as being an additional bonus for looking after his son. You weren't joking when you said that your clients were wealthy, sweetheart. That's a huge bonus…'

'But why did he send it to you?'

'He wanted to bypass the agency—he wanted this to be between you and him—and he didn't think you would send him your bank details if he asked.'

No, she wouldn't have, because he'd already paid her a bonus via Sabine, the standard amount Sabine had suggested as per the contract he'd signed. He'd paid her more—and for what, exactly?

She was going to kill him. She really was.

What?
Are You?
Playing at?

Bo grimaced at the three messages that had dropped into his phone a few minutes ago and felt the heat of Ollie's anger across the miles that separated them. Right, talking her round was going to take more effort than he'd thought.

Sitting in a taxi on his way to her parents' accounting firm in Wimbledon, Bo ran a hand over his jaw, wincing at the scruff beneath his fingers. He hadn't had the energy to do much over the past week, and shaving hadn't been high on his list of priorities. Neither had been eating. Sleeping had been impossible.

He'd spent time with Mat, and his little boy had kept him from climbing into bed, pulling the covers over his head and pretending the world didn't exist. But he had a company to run, an example to set and a son to be responsible for.

But work, once his whole world and his solace, meant nothing when his thoughts constantly went to Ollie, wondering what she was doing and how she was, whether she missed him at all.

Helen was wonderful with Mat, but she wasn't Ollie. Nobody was and nobody could be. Nobody made his house smell of roses. He missed hearing her laughter and her very off-key singing. He missed waking up with her, loving her at night—and in the morning, the afternoon and every minute in between. His life without her was miserable and bleak. When she left, she'd drained all the colour from his world.

He missed her. The guy who never missed anyone, who'd never allowed himself to feel, was pining for a woman.

It was no less than he deserved.

But, over the past few days, he'd realised that his current state of existence wasn't any way to live. Being apart from Ollie had made him realise that he wasn't his mother, cold and emotionless, that he couldn't view life the way she did and that not everything was a transaction. Neither was he his father: Bo had tried to flit from woman to woman and keep his relationships shallow and that had worked until Ollie had dropped into his life with her sparkling eyes and bouncing curls, bringing happiness to his cold, barren life.

It was as though someone had switched the light

on in his life and when she'd left—when he'd sent her away—the power to his world had been turned off.

He was tired of moping around, of being sad, hurt and lonely. If having her in his life meant marrying her, fully throwing himself into those waters, then that was what he would do.

Nothing was worse than being a walking, talking, flesh- and muscle-covered broken heart.

My girl's not happy with you.

Bo pulled a face at Paul's incoming text and knew he hadn't made a great impression on the man he hoped would be his future father-in-law. He hadn't even met the guy yet but he'd asked him via a video call—because he wasn't a complete moron—whether he could marry his daughter. Paul, dignified and quietly spoken, had made it very clear that, if he hurt his daughter again, he would bury his body so deep that not even Satan would be able to find it.

Bo believed him.

Paul had also told him where Ollie was and for that he'd be in his debt for ever. As long as he had Ollie, he didn't care.

The car approached the Cooper & Co building and Bo directed his driver to pull up before he reached it. As he did so, he saw Ollie flounce out of the building, irritation radiating from her face.

Right, she was mad. Well, she'd just have to get over it.

He got out of the car, slammed the door shut and

leaned his butt on the closed door, folding his arms as he watched her fumble in her bag for her phone. He shoved his hand into the back pocket of his trousers and waited for his own phone to vibrate. Yep, there she was.

'Olivia.'

'Don't you Olivia me,' she yelled, spinning away from a man who gave her a dirty look for her loud voice. 'What do you think you were doing, contacting my father and paying me an additional bonus through him? My parents aren't expecting me to repay my education costs and I can buy my way into Sabine's business on my own.'

'Call it a wedding gift,' he murmured but she was too angry to hear his heartfelt words. But, honestly, he couldn't wait to call her his wife... If he managed to get to the point of proposing without her ripping his head off.

'What do you think you were doing? How dare you contact my father? What do you mean it's a wedding gift?' she shouted so loudly that he could hear her from where he stood. Right, so much for the English sense of decorum. Olivia was missing that today.

Frankly, he didn't care. He could work with anger. It scared him far less than a studied non-reaction. Ignoring him would have meant that she didn't care enough to feel anything.

Heat was fine, cold was a problem.

'Argh! I cannot believe I am fighting with you over the phone!' she yelled.

'Well, you can fight with me in person, if you prefer.'

'I want to fight with you now and not have to catch a flight, Sørenson!'

'Your wish is my command,' he told her, lifting his hand to wave. He saw her look over at him, her eyes bouncing over the car before snapping back to look at him. She slapped her free hand on a slim hip and pushed her sunglasses up into her hair. Even from a slight distance, he could see that her eyes were narrowed. If anyone held a lit match to her, she'd explode like a Catherine wheel.

'Are you coming to me or am I coming to you?' Bo asked, keeping his tone reasonable.

Ollie looked around, her shoulders hunched up around her ears. 'I'll meet you at the entrance to the Italian garden in Cannizaro Park in twenty minutes.'

'Why don't you just get in the car and the driver can take us there?' Bo suggested, frustrated at being separated from her for one minute more.

'Twenty minutes, Sørenson,' she snapped. 'And, hopefully, that's enough time for my temper to cool.'

Right, okay then. He knew better than to push his luck.

Ollie stomped up to the low brick wall of the Italian garden, thinking that no man should look so good wearing a plain white polo-shirt, walnut-brown chinos and white trainers worn without socks. He looked as though he'd just stepped out of a cool, air-conditioned car—which he had—while she was hot and a little sticky from her mile-and-a-half stomp through Wimbledon. On leaving Cooper & Co, she'd pulled her hair up into a messy bun, but a few curls stuck to her neck and forehead.

She did not doubt that the little make-up she'd worn this morning was long gone and that she looked as frazzled and freaked out as she felt. Crossing her arms across her torso, she slowed her pace as she approached Bo, unable to believe he was in London. And, if he was here, where was Mat?

He answered her unspoken question. 'Helen, Mat and I booked into Brown's Hotel this morning,' Bo told her, handing her a cold bottle of water. She looked down at it and saw that he'd cracked open the lid for her. Hot and grumpy, and feeling as if she was a taut wire about to snap, she swallowed half the water in the bottle.

'Is he okay?' she demanded. 'Mat?'

'Mat is fine,' Bo replied, sitting on the edge of the wall and stretching out his long legs. 'I, on the other hand, am a wreck.'

Sure he was, Ollie silently scoffed. With his smart clothing and fancy watch, and expensive sunglasses over his eyes, he looked like the rich, urbane success story he was. Then Bo lifted his glasses off his forehead and pushed them into his hair and Ollie realised he was anything *but* fine.

The circles under his eyes were even darker than

hers and he looked a shade paler than when she'd left him in Copenhagen. And a few years older. Right, so maybe her leaving had affected him.

She was not going to think about his comment about her additional bonus being a wedding gift. He was being sarcastic, making a joke…he couldn't possibly have meant it.

Ollie rested the cool bottle against her hot cheek. 'What are you doing in London, Bo? And why did you give me such a huge bonus? It was totally over the top. You gave me a bonus when I left Copenhagen.'

'You know why, Olivia. Although your father is squawking that he will repay the money if you decide you don't want me, Ol.'

Want him? Of course she wanted him. The problem was that she wanted him all in, not just him dipping a toe or foot…

So he'd been talking to her dad—when? And for how long had that been going on? Bo stood up and came to stand in front of her, so close that the hand holding the water bottle pushed the fabric of his shirt into his hard chest. How was she supposed to think when he was so close and he smelled so good?

She looked up into his deep-green eyes. 'Can you give me some breathing room, please?' He had to move because there was no way she could make her feet step away from him.

He smiled. 'It's a big park, Ollie, with lots of space. All you have to do is take a step back.'

Argh! She tried, she really did, but her brain sent

the wrong signal and, instead of moving away, she placed her palm on his chest, stood on her tiptoes and placed her mouth on his. He was here: how was she supposed not to kiss him? Given the chance, she always would. Kissing Bo was what she was put on this earth to do.

Bo lifted his hands to hold her face as his mouth took a lovely and leisurely exploration of hers, taking his time to reacquaint himself with her. It was a kiss that said 'I missed you' and 'so glad you are here', gentle but with a hint of heat. Ollie knew that it wouldn't take much to make them spark and then burn. They were that combustible.

After a few minutes, Bo pulled back, wrapped his arms around her back and pulled her into his chest, wrapping her up in his embrace. He placed his mouth by her ear and his words were soft but powerful. 'Please don't leave me again, Ol.'

She had to be strong; she couldn't allow the wonderfulness of being back in Bo's arms strip her of her sensibility. She pushed herself back and his arms fell to his sides, disappointment on his face. Ollie lifted her hands to her face, mortified to feel hot tears on her skin. 'I can't do this, Bo.'

Bo gently peeled his hands off her face and, with the pads of his thumbs, wiped her tears away. 'Olivia, why do you think I am here?'

She stared at a spot below his size-thirteen trainer. 'Because you feel sorry for me? Because you want me to come back to Copenhagen to look after Mat, because you can kill two birds with one stone? So that you can have a lover and a nanny'?

He dropped a kiss on her forehead and his mouth curved into a smile. 'Sorry, but I'm not firing Helen for you. She's awesome.'

'She is?' Of course she was, she'd recommended her, and there was no one better to look after Mat. No one could do a better job…except her. Didn't Bo think she was as good as Helen?

'I have no idea what you are trying to say,' Ollie complained.

'And I'm making a hash of it because I've never done this before. I don't know how to tell a woman I love her, that she's my world, that I can't live without her. I don't know the words to tell her I'm a miserable, grumpy shell without her.'

With every word, Ollie felt herself lightening and brightening. 'You tell her like that, Bo.'

He looked surprised to find that his words had made an impression. Curling a hand around her neck, he looked down at her, his eyes warm with affection, desire and, yes, love—*woohoo*!

'I'm so in love with you, Olivia. Loving someone so much scares me but I'd rather live my life scared than live it without you.'

Ollie reached up to kiss him, smiling against his mouth. 'I love you too, Bo.'

Bo released a shuddery sigh. 'Thank goodness for that.' He banded an arm around her waist and hauled her into him. 'Now kiss me properly, Olivia. I've missed you so damn much.'

She would, she told him, but if they started to kiss they wouldn't talk, and they needed to. 'Let's just get it all said and done so that we can move on, Bo.'

Bo nodded and looked around. Spotting an empty bench, he took her hand and tugged her over to it. Thankfully, it was in the shade. When Bo sat down, Ollie put her hand on his thigh and turned to face him. She pulled her bottom lip between her teeth. 'Did you mean what you said earlier, about wanting to marry me? That the bonus money you sent my dad was a wedding gift?'

He lifted her hand and kissed the tips of her fingers. 'I did. I even asked your dad if I could marry you.'

Ollie's mouth dropped open. 'But you don't believe in marriage!'

'I do with *you*,' Bo told her. 'With you, I want the white wedding and the matching gold rings, the wedding contracts and the licence. I want more kids and to renew those vows on our tenth, twentieth and fiftieth wedding anniversaries. I want it all, Olivia, and you know how determined I can be when I want something.'

She did and every nerve ending was on fire thinking that *she* was what he wanted. But there was still one hurdle she needed to jump over. 'I can't be a stay-at-home wife and mother, Bo. I can't be someone who dedicates every last breath she has to her family. I mean, I will be the best partner I can be, but I want to work as well.'

Ollie held her breath, waiting for the anvil to drop.

He took his time answering and, when he did, his words were accompanied by an understanding smile. 'Of course you do, Olivia, that's why I said I wasn't going to let Helen go.' He ran his fingers up and down her arm, his expression thoughtful. 'When you were gone, I realised how wrong it was of me to expect that from you. I wouldn't want to give up my work, not even for you.

'You being a working mum wasn't an unreasonable request, Olivia, I just let my fear run away with me. I got the past, my parents' neglect and you tangled up and I was terrified of getting hurt again, of needing love and not getting it. I was being unfair and was more than a little ridiculous. I'm so sorry I made light of your dreams and aspirations. They are no less important than mine.'

His smile was soft and tender. 'I want you to have everything, experience everything, be and do everything that makes you happy. And, if owning an au pair agency is what you want, then you have my full support.'

He was telling her everything she'd so desperately needed to hear and nothing she'd expected him to say. He'd handed her the world.

And then he gave her a little more.

'And, if I need to pull back from my company, then that's what I will do. I can hand over some of my responsibilities to my managers and spend more time at home if you need to be in Paris,' he told her, sounding determined. 'You living there isn't ideal, but Mat and I can fly to you one weekend, and you can fly to us the next. We'll make it work,' he added. 'I'll do whatever I can to have you in my life, Ol.'

Her heart caught at the determination in his voice, the love in his eyes. 'Bo, I might need to be in Paris occasionally, especially at the beginning, but not on an ongoing basis. Most of what I need to do can be done online. The pandemic showed us that.'

'So all you'd need is a place to work?'

She grinned at his excitement. 'Do you think you can find a spare corner for me in your little house? You know, the one with the four guest rooms and the apartment above the garage in one of the most sought-after suburbs in Copenhagen?'

'Yeah, I'm not sure about that,' Bo teased back. 'Maybe you can work out of my closet off the master bedroom. Preferably naked.'

'Not going to happen, Sørenson!' Ollie hooked her arm around his neck and placed her cheek against his. 'Are we doing this, Bo? Are we going to get married?'

'We are.' He tucked a curl behind her ear and dragged his mouth across hers. 'I'm sorry I don't have a ring, but I wasn't that confident I could pull this off.'

Ollie laughed. 'Your standards are slipping, Sørenson,' she teased him. 'You only gave me the means to buy into a business I love and, far more importantly, your heart and your love.'

'And my son,' he reminded her. 'Will you be his mum, Ol? Will you be mine? Be ours?'

'Always,' she promised him. But always might not be long enough…

* * * * *

Were you lost in the intoxicating drama in
Hired for the Billionaire's Secret Son*?*

*Then don't forget to explore these
other stories by Joss Wood!*

The Billionaire's One-Night Baby
The Powerful Boss She Craves
The Twin Secret She Must Reveal
The Nights She Spent with the CEO
The Baby Behind Their Marriage Merger

Available now!

#4153 THE MAID'S PREGNANCY BOMBSHELL
Cinderella Sisters for Billionaires
by Lynne Graham

Shy hotel maid Alana is so desperate to clear a family debt that when she discovers Greek tycoon Ares urgently needs a wife, she blurts out a scandalous suggestion: *she'll* become his convenient bride. But as chemistry blazes between them, she has an announcement that will inconveniently disrupt his well-ordered world... She's having his baby!

#4154 A BILLION-DOLLAR HEIR FOR CHRISTMAS
by Caitlin Crews

When Tiago Villela discovers Lillie Merton is expecting, a wedding is nonnegotiable. To protect the Villela billions, his child must be legitimate. But his plan for a purely pragmatic arrangement is soon threatened by a dangerously insatiable desire...

#4155 A CHRISTMAS CONSEQUENCE FOR THE GREEK
Heirs to a Greek Empire
by Lucy King

Booking billionaire Zander's birthday is a triumph for caterer Mia. And the hottest thing on the menu? A scorching one-night stand! But a month later, he can't be reached. Mia finally ambushes him at work to reveal she's pregnant! He insists she move in with him, but this Christmas she wants all or nothing!

#4156 MISTAKEN AS HIS ROYAL BRIDE
Princess Brides for Royal Brothers
by Abby Green

Maddi hadn't fully considered the implications of posing as her secret half sister. *Or* that King Aristedes would demand she continue the pretense as his intended bride. Immersing herself in the royal life she was denied growing up is as compelling as it is daunting. But so is the thrill of Aristedes's smoldering gaze...

HPCNMRA1023

#4157 VIRGIN'S STOLEN NIGHTS WITH THE BOSS
Heirs to the Romero Empire
by Carol Marinelli

Polo player Elias rarely spares a glance for his staff, until he meets stable hand and former heiress Carmen. And their attraction is irresistible! Elias knows he'll give the innocent all the pleasure she could want, but that's it. Unless their passion can unlock a connection much harder to walk away from...

#4158 CROWNED FOR THE KING'S SECRET
Behind the Palace Doors...
by Kali Anthony

One year ago, her spine-tingling night with exiled king Sandro left Victoria pregnant and alone. Lied to by the palace, she believed he wanted nothing to do with them. So Sandro turning up on her doorstep—ready to claim her, his heir and his kingdom—is astounding!

#4159 HIS INNOCENT UNWRAPPED IN ICELAND
by Jackie Ashenden

Orion North wants Isla's company...and her! So when the opportunity to claim both at the convenient altar arises, he takes it. But with tragedy in his past, even their passion may not be enough to melt the ice encasing his heart...

#4160 THE CONVENIENT COSENTINO WIFE
by Jane Porter

Clare Redmond retreated from the world, pregnant and grieving her fiancé's death, never expecting to see his ice-cold brother, Rocco, again. She's stunned when the man who always avoided her storms back into her life, demanding they wed to give her son the life a Cosentino deserves!

HPCNMRB1023

HARLEQUIN
PLUS

Try the best multimedia subscription service for romance readers like you!

Read, Watch and Play.

Experience the easiest way to get the romance content you crave.

Start your **FREE TRIAL** at
<u>www.harlequinplus.com/freetrial</u>.